PROTECTING BRIANNA (SPECIAL FORCES: OPERATION ALPHA)

WATCHDOG PROTECTOR SERIES, BOOK 2

OLIVIA MICHAELS

Dear Readers,

Welcome to the Special Forces: Operation Alpha Fan-Fiction world!

If you are new to this amazing world, in a nutshell the author wrote a story using one or more of my characters in it. Sometimes that character has a major role in the story, and other times they are only mentioned briefly. This is perfectly legal and allowable because they are going through Aces Press to publish the story.

This book is entirely the work of the author who wrote it. While I might have assisted with brainstorming and other ideas about which of my characters to use, I didn't have any part in the process or writing or editing the story.

I'm proud and excited that so many authors loved my characters enough that they wanted to write them into their own story. Thank you for supporting them, and me!

READ ON!
 Xoxo
 Susan Stoker

CHAPTER 1

Brock "Badger" Jones heard the river before he saw it. The St. Vrain was riding higher than usual, thanks to a couple of back-to-back blizzards the winter before followed by a wet spring and early summer in the Rockies. The glacier-fed stream cut through the area's red sandstone, carving a path along a high cliff wall that towered over the town of Lyons.

Brock had meandered down to the river's westside bank after stopping by Riversong Coffee for a to-go coffee. He loved this section of the river best. Lined with apple trees, cottonwoods, and paved with flat red sandstone slabs, this stretch of the St. Vrain bordered an old farm that had been converted into an open-air concert venue decades ago. Watchdog had been hired to provide security for an upcoming music festival alongside local law enforcement. Brock was part of the security detail and as such he would be given a tour of the grounds and buildings.

But that was supposed to be tomorrow. Today, he was trespassing.

Not for the first time. The former SWCC—Special Warfare Combatant-craft Crewmen, Swick for short—was drawn to the wild river his buddy Sean Voelker used to talk about all the time, the river he'd grown up with. He'd talked about it like it was the mother of all rivers.

And maybe it was. Brock had certainly fallen under its spell. Since coming to Colorado in April, he'd visited the river as often as he could. Now that it was late July, the water was warm enough to enjoy for a brief summer window. Locals and visitors alike took advantage of the higher runoff to rent big black inner tubes and tube down the river, normally much lower by now and only good for wading in most spots, so he'd been told. He'd already waved to a few people happily floating down the river to the park where the St. Vrain widened out and calmed a little and they could get out and carry the tubes back upstream to do it again. Brock had put on swim trunks and a tee that morning with the idea of maybe tubing later.

Brock could hear people laughing and talking upriver. Their amplified voices bounced off the cliff wall. He caught snatches of music as musicians practiced their instruments a couple days ahead of the week-long song-writing class that culminated in a contest and performance at the very end of the festival. The hopeful musicians were staying in tents and RVs in a private campsite on the festival grounds. Their instructors—professional musicians in the folk, acoustic, and bluegrass scene—would mostly be coming in tomorrow to stay in the old stone farmhouse converted into guest quarters.

He smiled at their carefree laughter as it helped to elevate his blue mood. The voices helped bring life to the river. Brock walked toward the grounds around the bend. He'd stop just out of sight so that he wouldn't get into trouble. That wouldn't fly the day before he was supposed to be guarding the place. But he hoped to hear some of the music and listen to other people having fun while he watched the water and the ravens who lived in the cliffs above it.

As he walked, he noticed something resting under one of the trees. Curious, he checked it out. A violin case. *Did someone steal this? Or was it a practical joke?* Whoever it belonged to must be frantic. He picked it up, trying to decide what to do. Should he just give himself away and keep walking along the edge of the river, around the bend to the farm, and ask the group there who it belonged to? Or, should he circle around to the front office and give it to someone there? No way was he going to leave it here where God knew what could happen to it.

Better to seek forgiveness than ask permission. He continued along the river, his coffee in one hand and the violin case in the other. Maybe they wouldn't even know he wasn't supposed to be there.

Another tube came into view, and riding it was a vision of a woman. Strawberry-blonde braids under a straw hat, tanned skin, red bikini. Brock stopped in his tracks. He wasn't one to gawk at a woman, but Lord have mercy. He looked away quickly before he embarrassed himself or scared her and resumed walking as the tube drifted closer.

"Hey! Hey, you!" she yelled as her tube passed. "Stop!"

"What?" He turned to look at her. She was already

3

shooting past him, as this section of the river had some wicked rocks churning up the water and forming rapids.

She was trying to spin her tube around and sit up. "Stop! Someone help!" And then she was in the water.

Shit. Brock dropped his coffee and the violin and ran. The woman was paddling furiously toward the shore, her inner tube floating on down the river without her. The current was strong and carrying her away.

"I'm coming," he yelled as he ran along the bank to catch up, then splashed into the water, warm in the shallows but quickly turning colder as he waded in up to his waist. She was doing her best to reach him, moving at an angle toward both Brock and the edge of the river. She wasn't panicking—not yet at least—which would make his job a hundred times safer and easier. He pushed off from the bottom and let the current carry him to her faster. When he reached her, she yelled for help again and swallowed water. *God, now she's panicking.*

"Calm down. Let me help." He reached around her and pulled. The water was thankfully shallower here and she'd done a decent job of getting herself closer to the shore. The rocks were sharp and Brock was glad neither of them had lost their sandals as he stood and helped her while she coughed and fought him. Somehow, she'd miraculously kept her hat, too. The current let up as they moved toward the bank until the water was only ankle-deep.

She finally coughed out the last of the river and took a deep breath. "Get...the hell...away from me, thief." She high-stepped away from him as she picked her way between the sharp rocks to the muddy bank.

"Thief?" *Oh, shit, the violin.* "No, wait, I found it," he called after her as she sprinted upriver to where he'd dropped the case and his coffee. He ran after her, then slowed and put his hands up, realizing what he probably looked like. "I'm not going to hurt you. I saw it while I was walking and thought someone had stolen it. I was bringing it back to find the owner, I promise."

But she wasn't paying attention. She was too busy opening the case to examine the instrument inside. "The way you dropped it, I was afraid you'd damaged my baby."

Wow. Now he was getting annoyed. "I'm sorry, but I thought it was more important to save your life."

Her head shot up and her green eyes locked on his. "Save my life? I was trying to save my fiddle from *you*. I was fine!"

"Fine? You were calling for help."

"I was calling for help against a guy trying to steal my fiddle." She huffed out a breath as she looked at the instrument. "You're lucky she's not damaged. You'd better hope a Good Samaritan pulled my tube out of the river or you'll owe me the replacement fees."

Damn, really? "Well, you owe me for the coffee I dropped." Brock gestured at the empty paper cup lying on its side, its lid off.

She studied him. Head-to-toe looked him over. Her cheeks reddened. "I should turn you in to festival security. I don't think you're supposed to be here."

"I *am* festival security." *Well, technically. Starting tomorrow, but who's watching the clock?* he thought. "I wanted to make sure your violin—"

"It's a fiddle."

"Okay, your *fiddle*, wasn't stolen. That's part of my job." *Well, sort of.* "What's it doing over here, anyway?"

She sucked in her lower lip and popped it back out,

5

and damn was that hot. "I…didn't want anyone to watch me practice so I left it here. I don't like it when people watch me play." The anger seemed to drain out of her.

"Won't that be a problem if you're taking a music class and then competing in front of a crowd?"

"That's for me to worry about, isn't it?" She pushed past him. "Now if you'll excuse me, I have an inner tube to find," she said over her shoulder.

"Hey." He jogged to catch up with her. "Let me help."

"No, it's okay."

"I'm sorry about the confusion, but I seriously didn't want anything to happen to your fiddle."

"Thanks." She kept walking.

"I'm Brock, by the way. Brock Jones. My friends call me Badger."

"Yeah, I can see why." But she said it with a hint of a smile. "I'm Brianna Taylor."

"Wait." He paused and she stopped mid-step and looked at him curiously. "*The* Brianna Taylor, fiddle player?"

Her mouth dropped open and she frowned. "What are you talking about? Nobody's heard of me. I'm no one."

Brock grinned. "No one *yet*. So I just wanted to be the first one to say that before you win the contest and everyone knows who you are."

She made a scoffing sound as an incredulous smile spread across her lips. "You've never even heard me play."

"No, but I have a hunch about this. And my hunches are never wrong."

"Never, huh?" She arched an eyebrow.

"Nope. Just like I know we'll find your inner tube."

She rolled her eyes and started walking again. The

river was to their left and the ground to their right started to rise as they walked into a canyon that was carved around Lyons. A couple minutes passed before she said, "I'll buy you another coffee."

"I was kidding. You don't have to."

"Why? You didn't like it? Riversong, right?" She pointed up. They were about to pass under the bridge near the coffee shop in question.

"No, I love their coffee."

"You'd better because I work there, and I make a damn good cup of coffee."

"But not this week," Brock said, looking down at her. He'd been resisting doing that, because every time he looked at her it got harder to look away.

That got him a big smile. "Nope. Not this week."

"This week, you're Brianna Taylor, world-renowned fiddle player."

She shook her head. "'Badger' is right."

"Yup, I'm right."

She laughed. "That's not what I meant."

He was about to ask if she'd like to just skip finding the inner tube, climb the stairs on the other side of the bridge that lead to the street above and grab that coffee, when they spotted a couple of kids coming the other way. They were each carrying an inner tube slung over one arm and a third balanced between them on their heads.

"Do you know if someone lost this?" one kid shouted.

"Me," Brianna said. "Thank you!"

When the kids reached them, they bent and dropped the inner tube on the ground and started up the stairs to cross the town and drop back into the other branch of the river. They'd probably be at it all day.

"So," Brock said, grinning. "My hunch was correct. We found that inner tube, just like I'd predicted."

"Mmm-hmm." Brianna looked down at said inner tube while fighting back a smile. "We sure did."

"Because my hunches are never wrong."

"Whatever you say, Badger."

Brianna bent to pick up the tube but Brock beat her to it. "Here, let me carry that. And what do you say to that coffee?" He had another hunch she'd say yes.

"Um, I say that I don't want to show up at my place of business in a bikini with a fiddle, a giant inner tube, and a strange man right now."

Damn. "Oh. Okay."

"Why so glum? Wait...did you have a hunch I'd say yes?" Her green eyes glittered with mischief.

"No." *Yes.*

Brianna nodded. "Sure, because your hunches are always right."

"Well, you did qualify it with the words *right now.*"

She sucked in her cheeks and pursed her lips. "I did, didn't I?"

"So, I stand by my word that my hunches are never wrong."

She laughed and shook her head. "Okay, Badger, how about you take that inner tube back to the rental place for me for the trouble you've caused? I need to get to practicing. But," she held up a finger, "you said you're doing security for the festival, so I guess I'll see you around this week? Maybe at some point, we can go for that coffee."

Brock smiled. "Sounds good. And hey, I was planning on spending my day off today by the river. Would you mind if I came back and listened in?"

Brianna frowned. "I told you, I don't like playing in front of people."

Brock held up a hand. But, you've got to play in front of people at the festival, right?"

She closed her eyes. "Don't remind me."

"So, maybe I can help you, Brianna. Sort of a transition. I won't sit in front of you. I won't even tell you that I'm there unless you want me to. You'll have an audience, but you don't have to look at this ugly mug while you play."

Brianna shrugged, but her cheeks pinked up. "It's not *that* ugly."

Score. "So what do you say? In all seriousness, I won't if you don't want me to, because I'm not a creeper. I'll find a different part of the river to spend my day." Brock meant it. He was worried that he'd pushed her too far. But he really did want to help her. Sometimes, his enthusiasm to help someone overrode his better judgment.

She studied him. Then she nodded. "Okay. You know what? You're right. I have to break my cherry somehow." Her hand immediately flew to her mouth and she turned as red as her bikini. "God, I didn't mean that."

Brock pressed his lips together and looked away and he rocked on his feet. "Not gonna say a word."

She sighed. "Yeah, okay. Just let me know you're there so I don't freak out and we take this out of creeper territory. Then, just sit out of my view, and hopefully enjoy."

"Okay, I'll do that when I get back from this." He lifted the inner tube. "Question though."

"Answer." She grinned.

"If you don't play in front of anyone, how did you get

into the class and the contest? I understand the competition is fierce."

"Oh, that was easy. I just had to upload a private video so I set up my phone in my room and played. The headlining acts judged the final round of entries and I guess I made it." She shrugged. "The hardest part of that was working up my courage knowing some of my favorite artists were going to hear me. I mean, I don't know how I'm not going to die this week when I *know* they're watching. We're supposed to meet them too and I have no idea how I'll get through that."

"You're gonna be fine. No, you're gonna be *great*. Because I have a—"

"Hunch," they said together.

Brianna laughed. "I'll see you—or rather, *not* see you—in a bit?"

"You will." He gave her a wave and turned to go up the stairs, wondering if and how he could tell her that he knew one of the headliners personally through Watchdog.

CHAPTER 2

Standing beside the St. Vrain River, Brianna took a deep breath and shook her head, disbelieving the insanity of the situation she'd just put herself into. *Am I really about to let a total stranger who I met an hour ago listen to me practice the fiddle?* Granted, Brock was undeniably easy on the eyes, especially in a wet t-shirt that clung to his six-pack, and he'd proven to be a gentleman—if a bit pushy, but what did she expect from a guy nicknamed Badger?—but she'd never let *anyone* listen to her play. Now, she was standing there wondering if Brock was in place yet behind the trunk of the big cottonwood tree. He'd promised to let her know he was there without showing himself and she trusted (mostly) that he would do that.

Even though she'd changed out of her wet bikini and into a long skirt and crop top, she shivered. A tight knot formed in her belly as she picked up her fiddle and bow. She inspected them one more time, looking for any damage done when Brock had dropped them to 'save' her from the river. God, her heart had stopped and her blood boiled when she thought he was stealing it. It had belonged to her great-great-possibly-great grandma who had come West from Appalachia after she was orphaned, hoping to strike it rich or marry wealthy. Family legend had it that she played music in a local bordello until the madame fixed her up with a respectable man. At any rate, the fiddle had been in Brianna's family for generations and she'd had to sneak it out of the attic to play it. When Brianna was eleven, she'd spent her allowance and babysitting money from watching her younger cousins to get it repaired by the local luthier—re-strung, re-pegged, a few small cracks repaired—and back into playing shape. She wasn't about to let *anything* happen to her baby.

Brianna cleared her throat just in case Brock had forgotten to let her know he'd returned.

She heard a low chuckle that could have been attributed to one of the canyon ravens, except that it sent pleasurable shivers up and down her spine. Damn, not only was he easy on the eyes, but he had a great laugh.

"I'm right here, Brianna. I just got back. I was about to let you know but I guess my stealth skills aren't what they used to be."

"Oh, they are. I didn't hear you at all." She shielded her eyes from the sunlight reflecting off the water and peered at the tree. "Can't see you at all, either."

"I believe that was the point."

"Sure was."

"I also believe you're stalling. So git to fiddlin'," he drawled.

She rolled her eyes then realized he couldn't see her expression. "Oh, stop with the terrible accent."

"I'll stop when you start. What are you playing first?"

earned my trust. That just. Doesn't. Happen." She shook her head. "Truth is, I was just thinking about how you put me at ease and I'm trying to figure out why that is."

Brock smiled softly. "That means a lot to me. You can't imagine."

Now that *was a loaded statement.* "Wanna give telling me a shot? I know next to nothing about you."

Brock looked uncomfortable. He cleared his throat, and then looked relieved when the waiter came to take their order.

"What? Did I manage to out-badger the Badger?" Brianna asked when Brock gave no sign of continuing after the waiter walked away.

Brock laughed and blew out a breath. "You very well might have. Bravo, that's not easily done." He raised his glass in a toast. They clinked glasses.

"You're still avoiding my question."

Brock looked down, then straight into her eyes. Those crazy butterflies in her stomach fluttered. Finally, he nodded. "Okay. You're trusting me—which, like I said, means everything—so I'm going to trust you. Before I came out here, I lived in San Diego. I had my whole life planned out." He lowered his voice. I was SWCC, a Swick. Do you know what that is?"

"It's military, right? I guessed you were from the dog tags. But I'm not familiar with the acronym."

He nodded. "I'm not surprised. It stands for Special Warfare Combatant-craft Crewmen. We're a division of the Navy, handling small boats and supporting the SEALs. Can't tell you how many of their asses I've saved." He winked.

She started to laugh at his flirting, but there was a look

in his eyes, something that went much deeper. *He's covering something that hurts him with humor.* She put as much warmth as she could into her smile and asked softly, "What is it you really want to tell me?"

A look of surprise spread across his face. His mouth opened slightly and his gaze pierced her. His attention turned inward as he gave her the ghost of a nod.

"We had a mission go bad, rescuing a team of SEALs pinned down by insurgents." Brock swallowed hard.

Her stomach twisted into a tight knot. Had she pushed too hard, too soon? "I'm sorry. You don't have to talk about it if you don't want to."

"No, I do. You're just the first person I've talked to about this outside of military buddies and my family." His level of trust in her took her by surprise.

Brock went on. "I lost my best friend in that attack. He was like a brother to me. Sean Voelker."

Oh. Oh, goodness. Brianna nodded. "I knew of him but never met. He was older than me. His…death…was in the local news though. I'm so sorry you lost him."

He took a deep breath. "It's not just that I lost him, it's that I feel like it was my fault. I'd already gotten back aboard the boat with a casualty. I thought he was right behind me. He wasn't." Brock closed his eyes. "We don't leave our own."

Brianna's heart went out to him. "You had a man down and you had to think of that guy first."

Brock opened his eyes. "I've told myself that. Some days it helps, other days it doesn't."

She reached for his hand again. "Thank you. I'm honored that you would share this with me, that you feel like you can talk to me about something so important to you."

He grabbed her hand and squeezed her fingers. "It was...I've lost teammates before, but that did me in. I retired, wondering what I would do next with my life. I was living in San Diego." He paused. "Seeing someone casually."

Her heart skipped and her chest tightened. "Oh."

Brock shook his head, his eyes widening. He squeezed her hand again. "But we're over. We were over before I even left the military, I just didn't want to acknowledge it. Too much time away. And then when Kyle—my boss—contacted me to interview for Watchdog, she had no desire whatsoever to move to Colorado or to maintain a long-distance relationship. She said it felt like we'd been in one from the start and she was through with that."

Brianna hated the way she relaxed after that. It must have been hard on Brock, a second kick to the gut after losing his best friend. But, that left him completely single —available.

"That must have been so hard, to lose two important people so close together."

He gave her a tight smile. "It was." His smile softened. "Up until Sunday, when I helped out a woman in distress."

Brianna laughed. "Is *that* what that was?" Then she thought. "You know, actually that's true. I was in distress about playing in front of an audience for the first time and you definitely helped me with that."

"And again, it was an honor." He'd turned her hand over and was studying it, running his thumb along her wrist, sending pleasurable shivers up her arm. "You have no idea how good you are. How talented." He looked from their hands to her face. "How absolutely beautiful you are, especially when you play. When you're doing what you love."

She looked away, shaking her head.

"Brianna, look at me."

She shyly turned her head back. The intensity of his stare pinned her.

"I mean it. I know we just met, but I am absolutely captivated by you. I'm not going to lie and say I'm not. That's what I did wrong in my last relationship. I wasn't there—physically or emotionally—when I should have been."

How can he think that way? "But, you were serving your country *and* you'd lost your best friend. Any woman who couldn't understand that wasn't going to be right for you anyway. She's the one who should have been there for you." Her cheeks flushed with heat. "That's probably uncalled for, sorry. I never met her."

He smiled at her again. "Don't apologize. There's some truth in that, but it was on me to give her what she needed before it got to that point or recognize that it wasn't going to work sooner." Brock shook his head. "Look, she's in my past. My life has changed. I've changed—for the better, I hope. And what I'm asking for right now is the opportunity at a future with you. Whatever that looks like."

"I—"

He chuckled. "Just as I say I've changed, I see I haven't. I'm the same old Badger." He held up his other hand. "No need to answer now. You have a lot going on and I don't want to get in the way of that. Speaking of, as glad as I am that we're out together tonight, you need to be with the rest of the group, don't you?"

Dammit. I was hoping he wouldn't notice that. "It's okay."

"No, it isn't. I have a hunch that either Jerold is still messing with you or you still don't feel like you belong. Which is it?" A cocky smile appeared. "Because I can fix both."

Brianna grinned back. "Oh you can, can you?"

He nodded. "By telling you this. Brianna, you are amazing. You are way stronger than that asshole, way more talented, and a hell of a lot cuter."

That made her laugh hard. "I don't know, he's awful darn cute, don't you think?" she joked.

"More like just awful." Then he brought her hand to his lips and kissed it, raising goosebumps up and down her arms. "You are stronger than he is, I mean it. You deserve this. I know you've worked hard for it and have overcome a lot. I'm honored to be a part of that. Now, how badly is he bothering you?"

"It's not direct. There's just this...I don't know, menacing feeling that he's shooting at me like a death ray." She waved it off. "I'm probably being too sensitive."

Brock leaned forward. "Always trust your gut. But know that a guy like him is a coward. He's targeted you because you're the biggest, baddest threat to him there."

Brianna laughed again. "This?" She waved her hand down her body. "All five-foot-three of me?"

"No. This." Brock reached across the table and gently tapped her forehead. "And these." He took her hands and kissed each one, making Brianna cross her legs against the quickly growing ache those kisses induced. "It's your talent, and your sweetness, and your goodness that intimidates him because he has none of it."

Brianna. Couldn't. Breathe. No one had ever said

anything like that to her.

"Thank you," she finally said, her words barely a whisper.

"Thank *you*." He kissed her palm. "Brianna Taylor, world-class fiddle player."

"Keep doing that, and I'm likely to spontaneously combust, right here, right now."

Brock laughed.

"No, I mean it. People at the other tables are going to sniff the air, look around, and ask 'Who ordered all the fajitas? Oh, it must be that table over there that's on fire.'"

Brock laughed so loudly that people did look up as if there were a fire. When he finally stopped, he said, "Baby, that is one more thing to love about you; you crack me up. So, as much as it kills me—because now it *really* does—I'm gonna insist on you not going out with me this week if there's something else you need to be at instead. Don't let anything stop you—not some asshole, not any self-doubt." He grinned. "And sadly," he jokingly placed his hand over his heart, "not even dinner with me."

But that didn't stop Brianna after dinner when Brock walked her home from wrapping her arms around him and kissing him for twenty minutes before going into her apartment building. Luckily, the front light was out, and in the dark, they had all the privacy they needed.

The kissing started slowly—lips meeting, tongues tracing and exploring as they opened their mouths to each other. Brock left kisses all along her throat until she was practically swooning. She was moments away from inviting him upstairs when he pressed his forehead against hers.

"So damn hot," he whispered.

"We could go upstairs," she said.

"It's taking everything I've got not to take you up on your offer. But I know you've got a big day tomorrow, and if I go upstairs with you right now, I have a hunch you will get zero sleep."

She bit her lip and grinned. "Why do your hunches have to be right? It's not fair."

He cupped her cheek and kissed her forehead. "I will see you on the grounds bright and early tomorrow. I expect you to blow them all away again just like you did today. You've got this, Brianna."

CHAPTER 8

Ever since she'd made and sent the video, Brianna had awakened every morning with a jolt of nervous adrenaline to the heart. *Will the judges like my playing? What will I do if they don't?*

When she'd been accepted into the workshop, that daily morning jolt doubled in strength. *How can I tell my uncle I need time off to pursue a dream without seeming ungrateful?* She'd put off telling her family until the day before the workshop started, then muddled through that conversation, listening for the umpteenth time to her uncle talk about responsibility and the value of hard work. He'd finally relented, making her feel guilty that she was abandoning them, even though she'd pushed for him to hire extra temp help. She had not gone back to the coffee shop since.

On the first day of the workshop, that jolt of adrenaline had been so bad she'd thought of going to the ER instead. But gritting her teeth and reminding herself that she'd been through scarier, more uncertain times, she'd settled her heartbeat (mostly), grabbed her fiddle, and headed for the river.

And now this morning, she awoke to...a steady, calm heartbeat and Brock's words in her mind: *You've got this.*

Crazy how the right person believing in her could change everything.

* * *

"All right, folks," Anthony clapped his hands to get everyone's attention in the pavilion. He was with Brianna, Amber, and Jerold at the front so he turned to address the other groups of guitar, banjo, and mandolin players while the singer/songwriters took to the stage, Rachael in the lead. "We're going to listen to what the singers have been up to and then head down the block and into town for a break. When we get back, we'll be doubling down on practicing. Only a couple more days until the festival-goers get here and you have your chance to show them what you've got."

Brianna and Amber smiled at each other. They'd been bonding over their mutual love for the fiddle and as fangirls of Rachael's. Now from the looks of it, they had front-row seats to a private Rachael Collins concert.

Rachael stepped up to the mic. "Good morning! Hope you all are doing great today."

Everyone clapped and cheered. Movement at the side of the stage caught Brianna's eye. Jake was there watching his wife, briefly clapping before turning his attention back to the pavilion.

"After dinner last night, I don't think I need to introduce these two lovely ladies and one fine gentleman to you." She looked back and forth between the women on her right and the man on her left who joined her at the mic. "Especially after they killed it at karaoke."

Everyone laughed and Brianna felt the tiniest pang from skipping out the night before. Brock was right—she didn't want to miss another moment.

Rachael waited for the laughter to die down. "But I have to say that I won't be surprised when they need no introduction from anyone. These are three amazing talents and I have the pleasure of showing them off to you right now."

A look passed among the singers—little nods and smiles—before Rachael began singing 'Down to the River to Pray' and they joined in on the background harmonies. Brianna and Amber gripped each other's arms as chills ran down their spines. They sang like angels. Rachael stood back and let one of the other women take over the lead vocals for the next verse and so on until each singer had had a chance in the spotlight.

Wild applause erupted when they finished. They all held hands for their bow. As Brianna watched, she had the first warm and hopeful glimmer of knowing that she'd be standing there soon and listening to the festival-goers clapping for her.

You've got this.

When Anthony stood up, she glanced at Jerold sitting on the other side of him. A scowl was plastered to the man's face as he stared at Rachael, the same scowl he'd been wearing all that morning and the day before. Chills ran down Brianna's spine again but these were cold and unpleasant.

Amber squeezed Brianna's arm. "She's just *amazing*,"

she gushed. Brianna turned away from Jerold to smile and nod in agreement.

"All right, on that note, time for a break," Anthony said. "Instead of heading down to the river to pray, we're heading down to Riversong Coffee for a cup of joe. Sound good?"

Ugh! Brianna couldn't believe she'd forgotten that the workshop stopped by Riversong each year. How awkward was it going to be for her to walk in and act like a customer? Worse, what if they were truly understaffed? She'd feel compelled to go behind the counter and take orders. And if she went behind the counter, she might not come out again.

I can't. I'll just tell them I need to practice some more and stay here. It'll be okay. I'll go to everything else.

Everyone was standing and talking when Anthony announced that security from Watchdog would guard their belongings while they were gone, so they could leave their instruments. Just then, she felt a tap on her shoulder and turned to see Brock.

"I'll take that," he said as he picked up her fiddle.

"Oh. I…" She looked at the fiddle case in Brock's hand.

"Uh-oh. I have a hunch you were planning on skipping out again," Brock said. "Is that true?" His smile turned to a frown. "Do I need to have another talk with Jerold?"

"No, no." Though the mention of the man's name made Brianna look around for him. He was standing off to the side, alone, cell phone in hand as he stabbed out a text with his index finger. "He's not my bestie, but he's been leaving me alone today."

"Good. Then off you go."

"Yes, sir. Unless I could keep you company?" She

looked up at him through her lashes.

He laughed. "Nice try. You have no idea how tempting that is. But duty calls both of us." Brock pulled out his own phone and acted completely absorbed by whatever text he was sending.

Fine. Dang it, I hate that he's right.

Brianna picked up her purse and caught up with the rest of the group, her heart pounding and stomach sinking to the bottoms of her shoes. She practically dragged her feet as she walked at the back of the group. Maybe if she stayed back there she could avoid going to the counter altogether and her family might miss her in the crowd.

Fat chance.

She stared down at the road so she didn't notice when someone slowed down and started walking beside her.

"We missed you at dinner last night," Rachael said, startling Brianna. "Is everything all right?"

"Yes, everything is fine." Brianna gave Rachael what she hoped was a bright and cheery smile.

Rachael tilted her head. "You sure? It looked like you were ready to ditch us today too. And we're walking pretty slowly back here." She lifted her chin at the rest of the group, which had gotten a ways ahead and was just disappearing around a bend in the road.

"Okay, you're right. I almost did ditch." Brianna stopped walking.

Rachael smiled. "I knew it. Can you tell me what's going on?"

"Well, the coffee shop we're going to? That's my uncle's shop. He and my aunt basically took me in when I was a kid." Brianna decided not to elaborate on that. She didn't know what Rachael would think. "I've worked there since I was a teenager. They weren't exactly thrilled to find out I'd gotten into the workshop this week."

Rachael's eyes widened as realization dawned on her. "They didn't know you'd entered, did they?"

"No. They didn't even know I play." Brianna expected her to be surprised at that, but Rachael gave her a sympathetic smile instead, encouraging her to continue. "I don't share my music with my family because they'll take it away."

"Take it away?"

"My family has a history you could say. My uncle is trying to shake that off and he believes the way to do it is to work hard, not waste your time pursuing music. Doing that can attract the wrong people, lead to the wrong lifestyle." Brianna shook her head. "It's hard to explain. My family won't physically stop me, but it's more like..." She searched for what she wanted to say. "My uncle will give his opinion and it'll oppose mine, and his words will have the weight and gravity of granite beneath a city and my words will only be words. Flimsy and gone as soon as I say them. Dismissed."

Rachael smiled and nodded. "I had to hide my talents too. My father would have stopped me because he wanted to keep me low, to crush me, and the best way to crush a woman is to keep her from doing what she's meant to do." Rachael grabbed Brianna's hand. "It sounds like your uncle is opposing you out of love, trying to protect you. But the end result is the same. You have to stand up for yourself, Brianna. Trust that you know what's best for you."

"It's hard because he does love me, they all do. I feel

like I'm more a part of their family than I am of my own. My cousins April and Hannah feel more like my sisters some days. Okay, a lot of days. And I hate to say it but my uncle feels more like a dad to me, and my aunt like my mom. I don't want to let them down. They need my help at the coffee shop, and I owe them for taking me in all the times my parents were in trouble."

"Brianna, I know you feel like you owe them, but it's not like that with family—true family that loves you. I've come to learn that lesson since Jake came into my life and his family welcomed me without strings or conditions. Are you sure it's your family that's putting pressure on you, or is it you putting pressure on yourself to stay?"

Brianna laughed. "Maybe a bit of both."

"The sooner you get it figured out, the sooner you can keep doing what you love."

The knot in Brianna's chest that had been building since Anthony announced their destination loosened. "Thanks, Rachael. You've been a huge help."

Rachael grinned and chuckled. "Oh, it's completely self-serving. I just want to hear you play more. You have true talent, and I'm excited to see how far it will take you."

"Thank—" Brianna's words were cut off by the roar of an engine. A car flew around the bend in the road. It sped up, heading straight for them.

Brianna grabbed Rachael and pulled her back just as the car swerved at them before disappearing up the road.

"Oh my God!" Rachael covered her heart.

"Are you okay?" Brianna asked, her own heart pounding out an erratic drumbeat. She saw some of the group reappear around the bend, Jake in the lead and sprinting now that he'd caught sight of them.

"I'm fine," Rachael answered as Jake got to her and pulled her into a tight embrace.

"Dammit, angel, you are not to leave my sight from now on," Jake said. "Are you all right?"

"I am because Brianna saved me," Rachael answered. "She pulled me out of the way just in time."

Still holding Rachael, Jake's fierce gaze fell on Brianna and softened. "Thank you. Badger's right; you're something else."

Brock said that to Jake? Her heart fluttered. "It was nothing. Anyone else would've done the same thing."

"No, Brianna. Other people would have saved their own asses first." Jake stroked Rachael's hair. "I am in debt to you."

Brianna looked down at her feet as her cheeks brightened. By now, the rest of the group had gathered around them. Amber put her hand on Brianna's shoulder. "You okay, partner?"

Brianna looked up and smiled at Amber. *Partner.* That meant a lot to someone who was often overlooked at school at best, and teased and bullied for being who she was at worst. "I'm fine, partner." She hugged her newest friend.

Jerold stood there shaking his head, a look of absolute fury on his face. "What about me? I'm the one who's been wronged here."

Jake whipped his head around and stared the man down. "What in the ever-loving hell are you talking about?"

Jerold pointed in the direction that the car had disappeared. "That's one of my cars."

81

CHAPTER 9

As he stood in the Lyons police substation, Brock was so enraged he could barely see straight. Jake had contacted the rest of the team right after the near-miss and now Brock, Jake, Kyle, and Wolf crowded Sergeant Williams' office. Kyle's dog Camo stood guard beside the door as if they were about to be attacked any moment by a group of insurgents.

Williams drummed his fingers on his desk. "I'm telling you, we don't have a solid motive."

"Bullshit," Jake said. "Jerold Glass set this up. Rachael told me last night that he gave her the stink eye all through dinner whenever I was looking away. Hell, I caught him doing it and asked what his problem was. The little shit denied any problem but he kept it up today while Rachael was on stage. Stared at her like she was a bug he wanted to squash." Jake leaned forward and pressed his palms against the top of the desk. "You're telling me it was just a coincidence that not an hour before, someone stole a car off his lot and that same vehicle tried to run down my woman? It's *bullshit*. It's also bullshit that I'm even here right now while my angel's back at the festival grounds with that son of a bitch, but she insisted."

"Jake, brother." Kyle laid a hand on Jake's shoulder and eased him back up from the desk. "Go easy. George is on our side, trust me. He's a good man and I vouch for him, okay? So does Arden. Give him a chance."

Williams acknowledged Jake with a chin lift before returning his attention to Jake. "I appreciate that. Jake, I want to figure this out as much as you do. I don't like this shit going down on my watch in my little town." He settled back in his chair. "Glass's dealership is just outside of town right along the main strip coming in, and he keeps the used cars right up front, which makes it convenient to rob. Guy's a cheapskate and expects his salesmen to double as security, which of course they don't. Glass showed me the text his sales guy sent today describing the incident. The timestamp for the text and Glass's response correspond to the times on the video from the dealership and the call his sales guy made to my department. Two young men in baseball caps and bandanas walked onto the lot, broke into a 1972 Buick Skylark, and drove it off the lot in the span of five minutes."

Jake shook his head, unconvinced. Brock wasn't convinced, either.

"Hell, you can start those cars with a screwdriver," Williams said. "It was on the edge of the lot and the easiest thing in the world to steal, so they did and then drove like a bat outta hell. We'll probably find it trashed by the side of the road tomorrow."

Jake crossed his arms. "Not buying it."

Williams put up his hands, palms out. "The guy's a dick, no argument there. Always has been. But he's clean —well, as clean as a used-car salesman can be. Whatever grudge Glass might have against Rachael Collins, I don't think he'd go so far as to try and set up a hit, which is what this would be. His style is more like what you've described—a coward trying to intimidate with nasty stares and passive-aggressive behavior."

Wolf cleared his throat. "So, if Jerold Glass isn't behind this, who is? Jake, I imagine Rachael gets her fair share of weirdos. Anything lately or tied to the concert?"

Jake uncrossed his arms. "Sure, but we've followed up on a couple and they've ceased and desisted. Nothing lately, which makes Jerold look all the more suspicious to my mind."

Brock had been good—very, very good by his standards—but he couldn't hold back anymore. "Brianna was the target, I'm telling you." He banged on the desk for emphasis.

"We went over this," Williams answered, running a hand over his short, graying hair. "Same thing holds true. Glass is a bully, so by nature a coward who's gonna stick to tactics that won't get him in trouble. He wouldn't call a hit on Brianna because he's too chickenshit. I've known Brianna since she was knee-high to a grasshopper and that girl has no enemies. Some people talk about her disparagingly because of her family, but she's always gone out of her way to fade into the background."

"And now that she's shining her light for the first time, Glass has made her a target," Brock answered.

Williams stood up and came out from behind his desk, signaling the meeting was over, at least to his mind.

"Respectfully disagree that she was targeted today at all, let alone by Jerold Glass. If—and that is the biggest if in the world—anyone was targeted it would be Rachael, but my money is on a couple of punk asses out for a joyride. That sort of thing happens around here on the regular I'm sad to say, and this isn't the first time someone's stolen a car from Glass's dealership like that. Your women just had the misfortune of being in the wrong place at the wrong time."

Your women. God, was it that obvious that Brock was already starting to think that way about Brianna? Of course it was, the way he was standing here right now demanding justice for her. *My woman.* Those two words felt mighty good to him. Which was why he wasn't going to let this go. "*Respectfully disagree* right back atcha. If you aren't going to protect Brianna or keep an eye on Jerold Glass, then I will."

Williams' neck flared red. "Mr. Jones—"

Kyle stepped between the men and faced Williams at the same time Wolf pulled back on Brock's shoulder.

"George, it's cool, okay? Badger's just upset." He looked over his shoulder at Brock. "But he's gonna respect you as the chief authority in this town. Isn't that right, Badger?" He narrowed his eyes.

Brock huffed out a breath. "Aye, aye." Sure, he'd respect the fuck out of Williams so long as Williams understood that he'd better stay out of Badger's way when it came to protecting Brianna.

Wolf turned him and walked Brock to the front of the building and out the door. They stopped in the small parking lot.

"Brother," Wolf started, "I get what you're going

through right now, and believe me, this stinks to high heaven. But you've gotta trust we've got your back, okay? We're gonna be keeping an eagle eye on both Rachael and Brianna. Me and Kyle talked all the way to the station after we got the intel. I think Sergeant Williams is a good man but I also think he's blinded to the innocence of his little town as he calls it. I thought Rachael was the target at first too, yeah, but the more I think about it, the more I wonder."

Brock breathed out a sigh of relief. He'd been expecting a lecture on controlling his temper—par for the course. "Yeah, I wonder too." Should he tell Wolf about the white trash comment Jerold made to Brianna's face? It felt like a betrayal, especially after the conversation they'd all had at Arden and Kyle's place about Brianna's reputation. But her safety was more important, and besides, anyone who spent more than two seconds with Brianna could see she was anything but trash. "You guys think this has anything to do with Brianna's family? Considering their bad rep around here?"

Wolf nodded. "Yeah, the subject came up."

The men looked up as the front door opened. Camo took the lead and Jake and Kyle stepped out while Sargent Williams held the door open. "Give my love to little Ardie," he told Kyle, who laughed.

"You know it embarrasses Arden when her dad's old friends call her that."

"Which is exactly why I do it. Take care." Williams met Brock's eyes and gave him a chin lift. *Looks like Kyle's managed to smooth everything out* Brock thought. *But will he support my mission?*

He studied Kyle and Jake as they walked toward him.

Kyle said something, Jake nodded, and then headed off in the direction of the festival grounds.

"Wait up," Brock called and started after Jake.

"Negative. Get in my SUV," Kyle told Brock as he got Camo situated in his crate.

Oh, here's the lecture I was expecting. "Farm's only a couple minutes' walk."

"You're not going back to the festival. Now get in." Kyle gestured to the passenger-side of the vehicle as Wolf climbed into the back seat.

"But Brianna—"

"Is under the protection of Watchdog even as we speak. Now get the hell in the truck, Badger, that's an order."

Brock saw the wisdom in not fighting his new boss and climbed in.

Kyle started the SUV and backed out onto the road and headed east—away from the farm. *This just gets better and better* Brock thought. "Look, I'm sorry, Boss."

Kyle held up a hand. "Good start. But I also want to say that I trust your instincts."

What? That was unexpected.

"Williams is a good lawman, but in this case, I think he's wrong," Kyle continued. "Talking to both Brianna and Rachael, that car swerved right at them but didn't finish the job. Now, it coulda been a couple of dumb, joyriding motherfuckers who saw an opportunity to scare some women for fun. Or, it coulda been a warning."

Brock breathed a sigh of relief. "Kinda what I was thinking."

"I don't know if this Jerold guy is so hellbent on winning this competition that he would bribe a couple of douchebags to do in a rival, though it seems counterintuitive to take out one of the judges."

"Unless they didn't know who Rachael was. Maybe they only had a description of Brianna and knew where she'd be."

Kyle shook his head. "I'm perplexed, man. At the end of the day, all I can say is that I think there's more to this than a coincidence."

"Agreed," Wolf added.

"So, while Williams is gonna dismiss it, I'm taking the opposite side and looking at every possibility."

Kyle took a left and made a U-turn, sending them back toward the farm, Brock noticed. "Not even gonna attempt to tell you again to steer clear of Brianna, because—and stop me if I'm wrong—you won't listen to me anyway."

"Got that right."

"Yeah, I do. So hell, lean into it and see what you can find out—if there's anything *to* find out. But look, like I told you, I've seen how getting involved with a client can really mess shit up. So, I hope you appreciate that I'm threading a needle here. I know it's already happening so I can't shut it down and I'm not going to do the bullshit of turning a blind eye or having you deny the truth. But if I see it becoming a problem, I'm stepping in. Fair?"

Damn. Again, Brock was blindsided. "Aye, sir. Totally fair."

"And one more thing. I hear that surprise in your voice. You gotta know you can trust me, trust your new team, and that we trust you. I know it's a rough transition, going from military to civilian life, but we've got your six. And I'm personally grateful to you for giving my fiancée that last letter from her brother."

Brock's chest tightened. "It was an honor."

Kyle pulled up to the farm's entrance. Wolf leaned forward and tagged Brock's shoulder. "You've got this, brother."

"Thanks, man." Brock stuck his comm in his ear, exited the SUV, and headed for the gate.

Music permeated the air as Brock entered the grounds. If the other contestants were shaken up by the day's events, he couldn't hear it in their playing. Brock's body immediately relaxed in response, an effect he never expected. *If this keeps up, I may have to exchange my classic rock card for folk, country, and bluegrass.*

He followed his ears to the fiddlers who were gathered on a grassy patch under an apple tree, the sound of the river playing counterpoint to Amber's song. She was good, too, a worthy opponent for Brianna. Brock stopped a few yards away and studied the sour expression on Jerold's face as he watched Amber, waiting for him to cast the slightest glance at Brianna. But the man seemed to be aiming all his nastiness at Amber for the moment. *Equal opportunity dickhead.*

Brianna watched Amber too, looking enraptured by the music, but her posture told a second story. Her back was rigid and she sat on the edge of her folding chair. She had one leg crossed over the other and her dangling foot fidgeted like she was ready to run at a moment's notice. Brock could think of a thousand ways he wanted to soothe her anxiety, all of them involving a private room where he could slowly undress her, slipping the thin straps of her dress off her freckled shoulders, kissing a path down to her gorgeous breasts, listening to more of the sweet sounds she made when he did something she liked...

Focus he reprimanded himself. *This is exactly what Kyle was talking about.*

As if the heat of his thoughts caught her attention, Brianna looked over her shoulder and spotted him. He hadn't seen her since she'd left the farm for the coffee shop, hadn't communicated with her except through brief texts while she assured him she was all right but needed to give a statement. Now she smiled and waved her fingers before turning back to Amber. It killed him a little to see her act as though everything was fine, to try and hide her anxiety. She wasn't a soldier built to suppress that shit until the battle was over, but she was doing it all the same. His admiration for her grew.

Amber finished her song and the group clapped—even Jerold, though barely. Anthony stood and approached Amber. As he started giving her a private critique, Brianna took out her phone and started typing. A moment later, Brock felt his cell vibrate with an incoming text.

Hey! I promise I'm not ditching again but my family is twisting my arm to see them at the coffee shop before I go to dinner tonight with the group (believe me, I'd rather go straight to dinner). Would you mind coming along for moral support?

He looked up to see her watching him. She lifted her eyebrows, ducked her shoulders, and gave him a questioning smile and a thumbs up. He returned her smile with a wink and texted:

Absolutely I'll go with you.

Then he added:

Anything you need.

And hit send.

He watched her read her phone and loved the smile that spread across her face. It was like those first quiet, magic moments of the day when he'd be out on a boat during a mission and the sun rising up from the edge of the ocean lit the water and turned it into a carpet of diamonds. That always made him think anything was possible, and maybe—just maybe—today nothing bad would happen to him or his team.

When she looked up at him, her eyes sparkling, and mouthed *thank you* he prayed nothing bad would *ever* happen again. Not to her. Never to her.

CHAPTER 10

Brock insisted on driving the few blocks from the farm to Riversong Coffee before he realized what a mistake that was.

"No, huh-uh, no way." Brianna shook her head so hard he thought she was going to give herself whiplash. "I appreciate that you're thinking it might upset me to walk down the same street so soon, but this is my town and I'm not going to let myself become afraid of it."

Damn. Brock grinned. "So you're getting right back on that horse, huh?"

"I sure am." She carried her fiddle case in one hand and looped her other arm through his.

"I admire that," Brock said as they walked toward the front gate.

"Yeah, well. Let's see if you still admire me when I'm facing my family."

He stopped and turned, then cupped her cheek. "There is nothing easy about family."

"Especially mine. As much as I love them, they are tough customers."

Brock laughed. "And so are you." Not caring who saw, he bent to kiss her. Sweet cherry lips sent him reeling.

"Get a room!" They broke apart in time to see Amber passing and waving at them, a goofy, teasing smile on her face. "Am I gonna see you tonight at dinner, partner, please?" she asked as she turned and kept walking backward.

"Count on it," Brianna answered, beaming. "Just gotta check in with the fam first."

"Cool. See ya!" Amber turned again and kept walking.

Brianna waved and traded compliments and promises to be at dinner with other people as they walked. Brock felt her footsteps go from almost dragging to light and bouncing. And he thought nothing short of a nuke could remove the smile from her face.

"What?" she asked as she turned her smiling face up at him. "What are you smiling at?"

"You. At how much I've seen you change in just a couple of days."

Brianna shook her head, though her smile stayed in place.

"Oh come on. You're telling me you can't see it?" Brock waved his arm, indicating the other students and the farm. "When I met you, you couldn't even let anyone listen to you play. Now you're having fun with them. I love it."

"I have you to thank, big guy." She squeezed her arm around his.

Brock chuckled. "Naw. I'm just the doof who tried to steal your fiddle."

Brianna rolled her eyes. "You are way more than that." She pressed her cheek against his arm. "Thank you again for trying to commit larceny," she said with a dramatic sigh that cracked both of them up.

But as they walked down the street toward the coffee shop, her enthusiasm faded and her smile started to look forced.

"Hey." Brock pulled his arm loose from hers and wrapped it around her shoulders. "You've still got this."

"They're going to tell me to quit."

"And you're going to show them the same resolve you've had all day and they'll stop."

Brianna gave him a vague nod. They'd reached the far edge of the coffee shop's parking lot. Brock stopped and turned her to him. He kissed her long and slow. "I'm here for you."

Her smile returned. "Thank you."

Just before the dinner hour, Riversong Coffee only had a couple of customers plugged into their earbuds and staring at laptops, but the place was by no means quiet. Jazz played overhead as staff bustled around, restocking and cleaning before the evening crowd.

As soon as they walked in the door, a little boy with shaggy brown hair raced up to them. "I'm Kevin. Do you fart when you poop?" Before Brock even had a chance to open his mouth, the kid dashed off again.

Brianna covered her face with one hand. "Oh my God, that's my littlest cousin. He's five and slightly toxic."

"He's fucking hilarious, you mean."

"Ugh. Give him five minutes, you'll change your mind."

A woman with the same brown hair as Kevin's jogged up to them. She looked stressed. "What'd my kid say now?" she asked as she tilted her head over her shoulder in the direction Kevin had sped off in.

"Don't even ask," Brianna answered as she hugged the woman. "Brock, this is my cousin April. My other cousin, Hannah, is around here somewhere. Brock is doing festival security."

April kept her arm around Brianna's waist as she eyed Brock before extending her hand. "Nice to meet you."

"Nice to meet you, ma'am." Brock shook her hand. She had a grip as firm as the look in her eye. Protective. He liked that for Brianna on one hand, but on the other, he realized this was his first taste of what she might have to go up against to continue doing what she loved.

"So, how's the workshop going?" April asked her cousin while keeping her eyes on Brock. Her tone sounded too casual, especially in light of the day's events.

"Great. Brock's actually been a big help with my rehearsals."

April's eyebrow raised slightly before her expression snapped back to neutral. "Good. I'm looking forward to actually hearing you play."

"She's amazing," Brock said.

April shrugged. "Her family wouldn't know. She's never played for us."

Brianna rolled her eyes and stepped away from April. "You know how shy I am."

That made April smile and roll her eyes right back. "Really, Bri? You chat up the customers like nobody's business."

"Well, I'm not *fiddling* for them. That would be totally different."

"Uh-huh." A crash sounded somewhere behind them

and April and Brianna turned. "Crap, that's gotta be Kevin."

"I'll get him." Brianna jogged toward the sound before April could take a step.

"Thanks, hun," she called after her cousin. Then April turned back to Brock.

I have a hunch that here comes the interrogation.

April narrowed her eyes and looked him over. "So. You're festival security? Can you tell me what happened today? Rumor is my cousin was almost flattened."

How best to handle this. "Flattened is a bit of an exaggeration. I wasn't there, so I'll leave the details up to whatever Brianna wishes to share. But I will tell you this. From what I heard, she acted quickly and bravely and she has the admiration of Rachael Collins."

April gave him an accessing nod that was almost identical to Brianna's. Brock recognized a tactic shift when he saw one and braced. "She didn't mention that when I texted. Bri's pretty private. She hasn't mentioned you, either. How long have you known my little cousin?"

"We had the pleasure of meeting on Sunday."

"And she's introducing you to the family today."

"Yes, and I'm happy to meet you all." He lifted his chin toward Kevin, who was now getting a talking-to from Brianna. "Your son is a funny kid."

Her expression softened a little. "Thanks. I love the snot out of him, but I should've named him Dennis the Menace." She shook her head slightly as she blew out a breath. "It's a family trait on the other branch but it jumped to this one, I guess."

Brock tilted his head. "Family trait?"

April's eyes widened slightly. "Have you met...*any* of us?"

Uh-oh. "No, I haven't met her parents, if that's what you're asking. Brianna wanted to start with the coffee shop."

"*Just* her parents?" There was that little nod again, then April smiled. "Okay, well, good. Nice talking to you."

She turned but Brock wasn't done. "April, what are you saying exactly?"

Her shoulders slumped as she turned back. She opened her mouth but all that came out was a breathy *aahhh* as her eyes shifted back and forth. She snapped her mouth shut. "I..." she shook her head. "I shouldn't talk. I talk too much."

"April, please. You started to say something for a reason. What is it?"

April pursed her lips. "You don't give up, do you?"

Brock grinned. "It's why they call me Badger."

She crossed her arms and clucked her tongue. "Of course they do. No wonder Bri..." She glanced back at her cousin. "Okay, here's the deal." She shook her head again and lowered her voice. "Can't believe I'm telling you this."

"It's my winning personality."

April snorted but fought back a grin and stepped closer to him. "I'm telling you this for Bri's sake because apparently, she hasn't." She huffed out a breath. "Brianna is a twin."

Wait, what? Brock's heart stuttered. Maybe he'd misread her and they weren't as close as he thought if she'd failed to tell him something *that* important.

"Mmm-hmm. I can see she hasn't told you." April held up a hand. "Before you go getting your man-panties in a twist, don't be mad at her for not saying anything. They're estranged. She and Brian don't have that typical twin bond everyone is so fond of talking about. They couldn't be more opposite."

So, Brianna has a twin brother she doesn't get along with. "Opposite how?"

"Well, Brian didn't fall far from the family tree, while Brianna rolled away as fast as she could, right to our branch." April shifted her crossed arms into more of a self-protective stance than an angry one. "I love her like a precious little sister. And don't get me wrong, I'm fond of my aunt and uncle too. They're sweet people at heart and Brianna gets that directly from them. They just haven't always been on the right side of the law and Brian gets *that* part from them." They both glanced up at Brianna, who was now gesturing and shaking her head at Kevin, engrossed in correcting him.

Brock lowered his voice anyway. "Well, what kind of wrong side of the law are we talking about?" he asked, hoping to get April's take on Brianna's parents. "I mean, there's a broad spectrum between jaywalking and murdering someone."

"Oh, God, no, they've never killed anyone." April blinked rapidly. "Okay, well, at least my aunt and uncle haven't." She raised her hand again. "Joking. Exaggerating. Brian's never killed anyone. Gotten into plenty of fights, mostly because of his big mouth, but never seriously hurt or killed anyone. Though if he keeps it up, he might break my peace-loving aunt and uncle's hearts."

"Peace-loving?"

"Oh, yeah. So, my dad and Bri's mom were raised on an honest-to-God hippie commune, *not* joking. My grandparents were totally into that scene and had no problem raising their kids with peace, love, and happiness…and drugs. Lots of pot smoking and acid dropping there on the compound from what Dad's told me."

"Wow, so Brianna's mom was a hippie chick."

"Still is. *My* dad, not so much." She gestured around at the shop. "He traded weed for caffeine a long time ago and bought this place from the original owners about twenty years back. But my Aunt Luna's a grower and my Uncle Brian—also raised in the commune—was a dealer. Small-time, and mostly under the radar, though my dad had to bail them both out of jail more than a few times for that and other things. Brianna and Brian ended up living with us off and on growing up."

Brock's heart clenched at that. He couldn't imagine how hard it would be having to live with his cousins because his parents were in and out of jail. But just the idea of his mom and dad doing anything more exciting than Friday night bunko and bowling made him grin inside.

April dropped her arms to her sides. "Of course now that pot's legal, they've gone legit. They got backing from what's left of the old commune so now Uncle Brian runs a dispensary and Aunt Luna has an actual growers license with a warehouse and they're raking in the cash.

"Then there's Brian." She clasped her hands. "He's supposedly helping them with security but half the time he doesn't even bother showing up. I'm pretty sure he's stealing from them, too." She shrugged. "Not that I could prove anything. And it isn't really my business to pry or get involved, you know? Best we can do is that my family looks out for Bri since she has no interest in working there."

April looked over her shoulder. Brianna was hugging Kevin, then she stood up and headed back to them, smiling. "You didn't hear any of this from me," April added quickly under her breath. "I'm only telling you because Bri must trust you one hell of a lot to bring you here. Or she needs your help."

When Brianna reached them she looked from her cousin to Brock and back again. "Everything okay?"

April smiled widely. "Yeah, great. Just catching up with how you're doing."

"So, gossiping about me?"

April's eyes went wide. "Oh, no. You know. Just…talking." She shrugged. Brock tried to shift his features into neutral.

By the look on her face, Brianna obviously wasn't buying her cousin's terrible attempt at covering up their conversation.

Well, lean into it, Brock thought. "Hey." He put an arm around her shoulder. "Is that your uncle over there?" He nodded toward an older man behind the counter with his back to them as he stacked clean mugs on a shelf. The guy looked as big as Brock, though nowhere as fit.

Brianna looked up at Brock through her eyelashes, totally unconvinced she hadn't missed something important. She seemed to weigh something in her mind, but whatever it was made her decide to introduce him to her uncle.

"Yeah, that's him. Let's go say hi before he decides we're ignoring him."

Brianna set her fiddle case down on the counter just as her uncle turned around. His gaze landed on Brianna, love and concern shining clearly in his eyes before they shaded over with sternness. Without a word, he came around the counter, never breaking eye contact. She tucked her chin in and looked up at him through her lashes. Brock took a step closer to Brianna.

But when her uncle reached her, the big man opened his arms and folded her in. He closed his eyes and rested his cheek on top of her head. "We heard there was some trouble." He opened his eyes and it was Brock's turn to endure his stern gaze. Brock returned it with a friendly smile he hoped conveyed *no enemy here.*

Brianna broke away from her uncle and his gaze shifted back down to her. "Rumors of my death have been greatly exaggerated," she said lightly. "As you can see, I'm fine. It was just a couple of joyriders, that's all. Sergeant Williams is hunting them down right now." She turned and gave Brock a chin lift, acknowledging him. "This is Brock Jones—"

"Better known as Badger," April called over her shoulder as she walked by with a tray.

Brianna gave her the quickest glare before continuing. "Brock's working festival security at the farm, and he can tell you that I'm perfectly safe, can't you, Brock?"

Damn. Way to put me on the spot. But he brushed aside his annoyance realizing that if he didn't downplay the incident, she was going to have a fight on her hands. *And no one fights harder than a papa bear.* There was no mistaking that's what her uncle was.

"Sir—"

"Name's Sonny." He reached around Brianna to shake

OLIVIA MICHAELS

Brock's hand. Sure enough, it was like shaking a bear's paw, one that had come out of hibernation on the grumpy side and nothing at all sunny like his name. Brock did his best not to wince. Uncle Sonny must have been a linebacker in his day. It was damn near impossible for Brock to imagine this guy growing up in a granola-crunching hippie commune.

"Sonny…?"

"Taylor." When Brock glanced at Brianna, Sonny added, "My sister kept her maiden name and gave it to the kids."

Brock nodded. "Mr. Taylor—"

"Told ya to call me Sonny." He folded his meaty arms and lifted his chin.

"Everyone does," Brianna added in a soft voice that made him think she had doubts as to this going well.

No way to go but straight through. "Sonny. I'm just gonna get to it. What happened today is being investigated as a case of theft and they'll probably throw in a vandalism charge once Williams finds the car along the side of a road somewhere, which is what he's confident will happen. Brianna and Rachael Collins were just innocent bystanders, not targets. And this has nothing to do with the workshop. Didn't even happen there."

Sonny grunted and Brock got the message that he was now dismissed. The big man's eyes went from Brock to Brianna, who had looked increasingly hopeful as Brock spoke. "All the same, you left us high and dry here, Little B."

Brianna's face fell. She opened her mouth to speak as Brock silently begged her to stand strong. She glanced at him, closed her mouth, and blew out a hard breath through her nose. "Uncle Sonny, I love you. But with all due respect and love, I didn't leave you high and dry. You always hire extra help for the summer and around the festival anyway and I talked you into hiring an extra person this year, didn't I? I did that the second I heard I'd been accepted because I didn't want to leave you in the weeds. I wanted to make sure you wouldn't even notice I was gone."

Direct hit, though the big man tried to hide it. "How could you ever think I wouldn't notice you were gone?"

"I didn't mean that *literally*." She crossed her arms. "I just meant that you wouldn't be short-staffed. I didn't want to burden you."

Sonny snorted. "Now you think I resent you, that I think of you as a burden?"

Around them, Brock noticed the air growing taut. April had stopped working. Another woman, maybe between April's and Brianna's age and with a strong family resemblance, joined her. *That must be Hannah* Brock thought. With amused expressions on their faces, they stood watching the showdown, and Brock was tempted to offer them popcorn.

Brianna put her hands on her hips. "Uncle Sonny, please don't turn this around. You know I love you and Aunt Claire and that you've never treated me as a burden. You took me in without so much as a word of protest and made me feel like I was one of your own." She grabbed one of his big bear paws in both of hers. "You sheltered and protected me when I needed it, when my parents... when they couldn't." Her eyes filled with tears. "But some-times your protection feels suffocating. I appreciate the work you've given me here, I do. But I want to do *more* with my life."

"Don't you think I want that for you too, Little B?" Sonny growled. "I know you don't wanna be behind a counter your whole life pouring coffee, though you know I'd make you an equal partner just like I have for your cousins if you'd just say the word. But music? Of all things? Music ain't a life, not for most. Hell, hardly for anybody outside of teaching it maybe. Doing a gig in a bar on an odd Saturday night, or asking a coffee shop if you can play for tips, what kinda life is that? And the life*style*." Sonny shook his head. "That's the sorta stuff I got away from as soon as I could growing up. The military was the best thing ever for me."

He stooped and cupped Brianna's cheeks. "Your ma thought she was gonna be a musician too, but that just got her in trouble a few times. I don't wanna see you end up like my sister, God love her."

"She won't," Brock said. All eyes turned on him. Sonny straightened up and folded his arms.

"Brianna's got a once-in-a-lifetime chance here with the workshop and the contest. She's amazing. Everyone who's heard her stops in their tracks and listens. Not just lunkheads like me off the street, but real professionals who know what to listen for. She's got *it*, you know? She—"

"That's just the thing, we *don't* know," Sonny said. "She's never played for us. And we didn't know about you. Did you put her up to it?" He pointed to the fiddle case sitting on the counter. "I didn't even know she'd snuck that outta my attic. That's not good behavior."

Brianna rolled her eyes and threw her hands in the air.

CHAPTER 15

A nightmare. This has to be a nightmare. Brianna tucked her body tighter as she felt the van swerving. Sobs and prayers filled the van but she stayed as cool as she could. *Jake's got us. And Brock won't let anything happen to me.*

Then the van hit something hard and the world went sideways. There was a brief moment of stillness before the van hit again and they stopped at a weird angle—the nose of the van pointing down and tilted, not quite on their side. The engine died and the distant sound of rushing water and birdsong filled the air, shocking in its tranquility.

Brianna raised her head. The air was filled with smoke or dust, and it smelled funny. She wasn't hurt, or at least she felt no pain—yet. She looked around at the other passengers who were coming out of their crash positions. Sitting next to her, their singer, Twila, grimaced and gripped her door-side shoulder. "I think it's dislocated," she whimpered.

Brianna looked between the front seats where Jake

and Rachael sat. They weren't moving. The airbags had deployed—filling the van with their dust, she realized—and Brianna prayed her friends had only been stunned or knocked out. She started to undo her seatbelt to help them when the van righted itself and rolled forward. Everyone gasped and screamed for the eternally long moment before the van stopped again with a hard thud. Brianna figured they must have lodged against some rocks or a boulder, but with the heavy storms the area had gotten over the spring, the rain-loosened rocks could shift at any moment and send them into the water below. *And God forbid if the van flipped over on the way down…*

"No one move," she said as calmly as she could. "Sound off; who's awake and how are you? This is Brianna and I seem to be okay."

"Twila." Her voice was breathy, full of pain. "Shoulder definitely dislocated."

One by one, every person in the back gave their names and conditions. Besides Twila, only minor bumps and bruises, thank goodness.

"Rachael? Jake?" Brianna called. "Report?"

Rachael stirred, thank God. "Jake?" she said. Brianna watched her reach across the gap and touch his arm.

Nothing.

Then he groaned. "Shaken, rattled, and rolled, but still in one piece. Angel, how are you?"

"Same, but I hit my head."

Jake started to move and Brianna said, "No! The van's not stable," just as it rocked.

"All right, everyone stay calm and stay still," Jake said. "Badger, come in." Jake's voice sounded a little slurred to Brianna. Rachael must have noticed too, judging by her worried face. "Copy, Badger. No fatalities, minor injuries, possible concussions, one dislocated shoulder. Me, I'm a bit woozy. But the van wants to take a swim so we need to get the fuck outta here ASAP."

Okay, so Jake could communicate with Brock, which was a good thing. He'd save them, Brianna had no doubt. *But tell that to my heart* she thought as it jackhammered against her rib cage. Did she hear a distant siren? Over the sound of rushing water, it was hard to tell if it was wishful thinking or real. She closed her eyes and focused. Yes, a siren. But better than that, Brock's voice somewhere above them shouting orders.

"I can't do this," Twila whimpered next to her. Her tan face was quickly losing color and her breathing was quick and shallow.

"We're gonna be okay," Brianna whispered to Twila, who gripped her hand. "Just breathe with me, okay? You're a singer, you know how to breathe deeply, right? Let's do it." Brianna took a deep breath and held it, nodding encouragement to Twila as she blocked out her own fear. Twila breathed in and they exhaled together. Twila matched Brianna's next two breaths as color returned to her face. And damn if Brianna didn't feel a little calmer herself.

Then she heard the best sound ever—Brock's voice, just outside the rear of the van.

"Everyone, we're going to get you out. We need to stabilize the vehicle and then we're going to use ropes and litters to get you back up the hill. I will let you know when it's safe to move and then we'll be evacuating from the back of the van to the front. The way you can help me in the meantime is I need everybody to stay calm and stay still."

"Calm and still," Twila repeated as sweat trickled down the side of her forehead. Brianna squeezed her hand and prayed that Brock wouldn't slip and fall to his death. With the AC off, the air in the van was growing warm and stale, smelling of sweat and fear.

The van shifted and slid. Everyone gasped. Brianna fought the urge to shout Brock's name, to tell him that despite the fact they'd just met, she loved him. She'd never known anyone so brave, so big-hearted, so gentle and yet so strong. He'd made her feel protected yet brave too, and seen in a way that didn't hurt and humiliate. He accepted her despite her bad blood. Brock had helped her find her way to her music and that's all she'd ever wanted in a partner—wanted, and never expected to find.

The van stopped sliding again. Everyone breathed out a collective sigh of relief.

Please, Brock. Please hurry so that I can tell you I love you.

The siren had cut out without her realizing it. She wondered how many vehicles had come to the rescue. She listened to Brock give directions to the other two guards about securing the van, and she listened to Jake's updates. She held Twila's hand and breathed with her. And in the back of her mind, the refrain repeated—*I love you, I love you, I love you.*

The late-afternoon orange sunlight had faded to purple twilight by the time the back doors opened. Brianna turned and saw the best sight ever—Brock's face looking in, his eyes searching until they landed on her.

"We're going to start the evacuation process now," he said right to her. "Starting with the rear. We're going to go slow and careful. The van is as stabilized as it's gonna get and we're gonna keep it that way. Listen to me and do exactly as your told and you're going to be fine." He held her eyes a moment more before turning to the mandolin player and helping him out of the van. He was wearing shorts and his knee was banged up and bleeding but he seemed to be moving all right. He slung his mandolin case over his shoulder on its strap.

Next was the guitarist who thanked Brock profusely as he helped the man out of his seat. Then the singing instructor, who clung to him in a way that sparked the tiniest bit of possessiveness in Brianna. If she didn't already like the woman, she'd probably do something stupid and ill-advised once Brock got Brianna out and standing on the road above.

After Brock made sure the banjo player was secured, it was Brianna's turn. She watched Brock make his way carefully down the aisle between the seats, his gaze never leaving hers, lending her strength. It wasn't until he was close that she saw the fear in his eyes.

"Brianna, are you all right?"

She nodded. "But Twila needs help. She's in terrible pain. Help her first."

He closed his eyes briefly and then opened them on a huff. "All right, Twila. Let Brianna help you out of the seatbelt and I'm going to get you to safety. We've got EMTs up there looking everyone over. Mighty good pain pills I've heard."

Twila gave him a half-smile. "The ibuprofen Bri gave me was great but I think it's wearing off."

"Then let's go."

Brianna helped get Twila out of her seat and Brock

half-carried her to the back of the van. The extra minutes he was gone and helping Twila into a litter were the longest of Brianna's life. Finally, Brock reappeared and moved quickly to her.

"All right, baby, *your* turn." He gave her the quickest kiss on the cheek.

"Do I get one of those?" Jake asked.

"Only if you ask nice," Brock said with a smirk. He had Brianna standing, and now that she was moving she started to feel pain and stiffness here and there.

"In that case, I'm not waiting." Jake undid his buckle and reached for Rachael's. "We're getting out of here now, angel."

"You all right to do that, brother?" Brock asked.

"Hell, yeah. Badge, I know you did a great job stabilizing this thing, but enough's enough. I'm not waiting around another second." Brianna heard him helping Rachael behind her as Brock helped her to the back of the van.

Which shifted enough to send Brianna to her knees with a cry of fear.

But the van held.

"It's okay, baby, probably just a rock in front giving way. It's still secure."

When she got to the opening, she saw what Brock meant. Chains snaking back up the hill to the road above kept the van from sliding. Brock grabbed her hand and put it on a taut rope.

"Grab that rope with both hands and use it to help you climb to the litter." It was only a few feet above them on a flatter ledge, but the angle of the ground between had to be at least forty-five degrees.

Brianna suddenly felt her strength ebbing away. All she wanted to do was curl up like a small animal and stay right there. *No, no, you're not doing that, Bri. Get ahold of yourself. Just a little farther. You've got a contest to win.* She nodded at Brock, grabbed the rope, and climbed to the litter where Mack waited. Brock was right behind her, so if she did slip, she'd fall into a solid wall of Swick.

Smiling, Mack said, "There she is," as if he were waiting in a restaurant and just caught sight of her at the door. He gripped her arm and helped her up. Brock quickly secured her in a litter and up she went. Below, she heard Rachael getting the same treatment.

As the litter rose, the day got brighter again. It wasn't as late as she thought but they were far down enough that the setting sun couldn't reach them. She tried to focus on that instead of the realization that she was hanging above a ravine and had come this close to losing her life. Would they pull the van up after everyone was safe, or let it fall? She imagined it turning over in space and felt sick to her stomach.

And then the real nausea hit. She'd been so focused on helping Twila, and then so relieved to see Brock...

"Oh my God. My fiddle. I left my fiddle." Her beloved fiddle, her family's heirloom, the one that belonged to her great-great-great-grandmother—her prized possession brought out West. There was no way she'd get it back in time for the performance tomorrow. What if the van did fall into the river in the meantime? *Gone forever.* Brianna bit her lip to keep from crying. *Be thankful you're alive. Just be thankful you're alive and focus on Brock and everyone else down there getting back up the mountain safely. That's what's important.*

I'm not going to cry.

Flint and another man were standing by at the top of the mountainside. They grabbed her litter and pulled her up over the guard rail and onto the road where they helped her out of it. Flint was talking to her but she couldn't focus on his words so she just nodded until he tried leading her toward a waiting ambulance where EMTs were checking the others out.

"No. I have to make sure Brock is okay." She went back to the guard rail and looked down. Vertigo hit as she realized just how steep the mountain was, how precarious her situation had been. She gripped the edges of the railing as she watched Rachael's litter swing and the three men climbing the ropes beside it.

Flint grabbed her and gently pulled Brianna away from the railing. "Whoa, there. Looked like you were gonna go right back over the side. They're okay, I promise." He pressed a bottle of water into her hands. "Drink this, it'll help."

She looked at the bottle. Flint took it back out of her hands and unscrewed the top for her. "Here you go."

"I'm sorry," she said. "I'm not dumb, I'm—"

"Just in a little bit of shock, sweetheart, I know. We need to get you over to the paramedics, okay?"

"Please, can I wait here until they're safe? I'm okay now, I promise."

Flint studied her eyes for a moment. "All right, but you're standing back here with me."

Just then, Amber ran up to them. "Honey, are you okay?" She hugged Brianna. "We've all been so worried."

"I'm fine, but my…" She gestured helplessly toward the ravine. "I left my fiddle in the van."

Amber's hand flew up to cover her open mouth. "Shut the front door, you did not!" She looked as crushed as Brianna felt right now.

Brianna nodded, fighting back tears at Amber's expression.

"I know you'll get it back, honey. Listen, my fiddle isn't the greatest, but since we're on at different times, you borrow mine for tomorrow."

That did it. The first tears streaked down her cheeks. "Thank you." She could barely get the words out around the lump in her throat. To think this woman had been a complete stranger just a few days before, a competitor, and was doing something this nice for her. It broke her heart in the best way.

"Well, I doubt Jerold would be willing to lend you his," Amber said, rolling her eyes. She looked around. "I don't even know where he is. We're supposed to stay close since it's gonna get dark soon."

Flint jogged the few steps back over to the guard rail as Rachael's litter came into view. He and the other man helped her out of the litter as Jake and Mack climbed up— Mack giving Jake a hand—followed by Brock.

"Oh thank God!" Brianna rushed to Brock and he stretched his arms out for a hug. Brianna wrapped her arms around him and he held her tightly.

"Hang on," he said as he let her go. He shrugged out of a backpack and unzipped it. "I think you're gonna need this."

"My fiddle!" Brianna burst into tears as she took her beloved instrument from Brock. "Oh my God, you risked your life to get it."

"Saved it for real, *this* time," he said, nuzzling into her hair.

"*And* me. For real, and again." She looked up into his face. His eyes had gone soft and warm, his head slightly tilted as he gazed back down at her. "I love you, Brock. I know it's crazy-early to be saying that, but time is short and precious, and—"

His lips claimed hers in a hard, hot kiss. She moaned into his mouth as love and relief surged through her. She was safe in his arms where she belonged and he knew she loved him. She couldn't ask for more.

And yet he gave it to her. He eased their kiss to a stop and cupped her face in his hands. "I love you too, Brianna. From the moment I saw you, I loved you. How's that for crazy-early, baby?"

She grinned. "I'll take it."

"Yeah, you will." He kissed her again and the rest of the world faded away like the last high note at the end of a song. There were only the two of them in the entire world.

"Now," he whispered against her lips. "Let's get you checked out with the EMTs."

Brock and Brianna turned and started toward the ambulance when Flint stopped them.

"We have a situation," he said. "Jerold Glass is gone."

CHAPTER 16

Brock stiffened, rage taking over the happiness he'd just felt at Brianna's words. "Are you fucking kidding me? I'm damn sure he's behind this." He cupped Brianna's face quickly before letting her go and turning to address the situation. "Someone get her to an EMT. Where's my dog?" He sprinted to the SUV. He'd opened the doors to give Valkyrie air while he was helping with the rescue. She waited patiently in her crate but now her body went taut with expectation. Brock released her and took out the plastic bag he'd stuffed in his pocket earlier. He unzipped the top and let the dog get a whiff of Jerold's scent.

Then he commanded her to track.

They ran as fast as Brock could go, farther down the road toward Lyons. Sure enough, Brock saw a figure up ahead at the next pull-off, waiting in the shadow of the trees.

"Glass! What are you—"

As soon as he spotted Brock and Valkyrie, Jerold took off running.

Stupid motherfucker. Brock unhooked Valkyrie and gave the command to catch and hold, the way Alex had trained him and the rest of the guards at Watchdog. The dog quickly shortened the distance. Jerold yelled and put on speed—to little effect.

"Just stop running," Brock shouted. The idiot was in no shape to be outrunning a Malinois trained to catch and hold a combatant, and a former Swick used to running six to ten miles every day.

Jerold stopped and turned. *At least the dumb asshole has that much sense.* Except the insane grin on his face said otherwise.

Time slowed as Brock watched Jerold pull out his gun, then aim it straight at Valkyrie.

Brock reached for his P228 Sig. "Wouldn't do that."

"Then call it off!"

Valkyrie slowed but didn't stop.

"Drop your gun, Glass."

"Fucking *call it off!*"

"Drop. Your. Gun." Brock aimed for Jerold's head.

A car engine grew louder, coming up the hill. *Fuck.* "Valkyrie, heel!" The dog spun around and ran back toward Brock.

Jerold pulled the trigger.

Asphalt chips and dust flew up beside Valkyrie, who doubled her speed. Jerold raised his gun and pointed it at Brock.

The car sped into view and did the stupidest thing ever—pulled a U-turn between Valkyrie and Jerold and stopped. A new, plateless Dodge Charger, probably straight off Jerold's lot.

"Bitch! What the fuck took you so long?" Still pointing

the gun at Brock, Jerold threw the passenger-side door open and jumped in. They sped off toward Lyons.

Valkyrie reached Brock as he pulled out his cell and started jogging back to the others. When Sergeant Williams answered, Brock said, "Sergeant, Brock Jones here at—" He passed a mile marker, turned, and read it off. "Glass is headed toward Lyons." He gave a quick description of the Dodge. "Consider him armed and dangerous, probably coked up and I'll drop off proof of that. Crazy son of a bitch took a shot at my dog and aimed at me. You'll find a divot in the pavement and the casing just on the other side of the pull-off here. Among other things, you're gonna want him for questioning in this so-called van accident."

A minute later, one of the police cars at the site of the crash flew past him, sirens wailing.

When he got back to the site, twilight was descending in earnest. Flashing red and blue lights reflected off the red cliff walls below the last of the daylight. A second cop car took off slowly down the hill, probably to check out the sight of the shooting. Jerold Glass was somebody else's problem now and Brock had no doubt they'd catch him pretty quick—the road followed the South St. Vrain and there weren't more than three or four turn-offs between here and Lyons. God help the woman he'd conned into aiding him. Brock would give the baggie over to Williams or whoever was still there and be done with it for the night.

Because he had more important things to do.

Brock picked up his pace when he made out Brianna's outline near the ambulance. She started toward him. In the shadows, he couldn't make out her features but everything about her body language said she was tense and worried. She clutched her fiddle case like a baby.

Brianna bent stiffly and scratched Valkyrie's head, then she straightened and asked, "Was that a gunshot? Everyone is saying it was a gunshot."

He put his arm around her and pulled her close. "Ongoing investigation and not your concern right now, baby." He kissed the top of her head as they walked back. "My first concern is how are you? The EMTs give you the all-clear?"

Brianna nodded. "They said I'll probably be stiff in the morning, like everyone else, which sucks since we have to play. But the other two groups are happy to switch the schedule around so that we go on last, which is cool. The EMTs gave me a couple muscle relaxants if I need them, but I don't want to feel fuzzy-brained." She grimaced. "I avoid any pills stronger than aspirin."

"So, that calls for a thorough massage later." He felt her shiver and grinned. "You suddenly cold, baby?"

She grinned back. "More like suddenly hot."

"You're always hot." He kissed her again, liking this line of conversation better.

But it didn't hold. "Seriously, what happened down there? Did he fire that damn gun? He's been a little extra scary all day. And," she lowered her head, "trying to tell anyone who would listen that it's all because of me and my family."

Brock stopped and turned her in his arms until she was facing him. "Brianna, I want you to look around, right now."

"Okay." She did as he asked. "What am I supposed to

see besides an ambulance, some vans, and a tow truck trying to pull out the van that nearly killed me?"

He sighed and shook his head at her smart-aleck response. "*Babe*. The people. I'm talking about the people."

"All right, I see my fellow contestants. I see Amber trying to work up the nerve to approach Rachael and ask if she's okay. I see Twila wearing a sling. I see the guys from Watchdog."

"Yeah. You see *friends*. Everywhere you go, Brianna, it's like there's a light shining around you. Twila would've been a panicky woman in a lot of pain and probably in my way if you hadn't helped her. The entire van would have been a hot mess without you, actually."

"Not true. I didn't do anything."

"No, *that's* not true. You took charge while Jake was still seeing little cuckoo birds circling his head."

That got him a laugh.

"You asked how everyone was so he could give report, and that also kept everybody calm and focused in the first crucial moments and set the tone for the entire rescue. Do you know how important that is? You're a hero, babe, and everyone here knows it."

She started to protest and he stopped her. "What you *don't* see is anyone who believes the bullshit about you that Jerold was trying to spread. They know who you are and who he is. Tomorrow, they'll learn more." He turned her again and headed for the SUV. "I'm going to keep hammering at you until you see the world as it is—one that isn't judging you harshly all the time. One that sees the same light that I see."

She opened her mouth and closed it again.

"What?"

"I love you. That's all."

Damn if that didn't make his heart race. He cupped her face in both hands and pressed his forehead gently but firmly against hers. "Love you, too. So much."

He reluctantly pulled away. "You're riding down with me." He opened the passenger-side door to his SUV and helped her in. "Now, I need to make sure everyone else is cleared for travel and get them divvied up among the other two vans and my truck. And then I'm taking you home." His cock pulsed, seeing the hungry look in her eyes. He leaned in and kissed her fast and hard, savoring the few seconds of contact.

He crated up Valkyrie, gave her a Kong with extra peanut butter stuffed inside, and heaped praise upon her furry head before shutting the door. "Thanks for the help today, girl, but tonight, you're back at Watchdog. I know Alex and Kyle are both gonna baby you."

Twenty minutes later, they were back on the road. An hour after that, Brianna was in his arms again—and this time he had no intentions of stopping.

CHAPTER 17

Brianna led Brock up the flight of stairs to her apartment, her legs shaking and her heart doing its best to escape the confines of her chest. She didn't think there was one unfelt emotion left in her body after the day she'd had. By all rights, she should've been exhausted, but instead, she'd never felt more awake and alive.

And God, did she need Brock to help her burn off some adrenaline.

Her hands trembled as she tried to fit the key into her lock. She giggled at the whole phallic situation until Brock caught on and started laughing too. He finally grabbed her keys and inserted the right one into the lock.

"A preview?" She barely got out the words before she was back in hysterics.

"Someone is squirrelly," he growled in her ear. "Better work off some of that energy, huh?"

The minute her door was open, Brock had her up against the wall. His mouth came down over hers— relentless, demanding, claiming her until she was moaning helplessly into his mouth. He gripped her wrists and slid her arms up over her head as his hard body pressed against hers. She wrapped her right leg around his waist and used it to pull him even closer, savoring the feel of his erection pressing against her clit. She couldn't remember the last time she'd even had sex, let alone wanting someone this much. She rubbed herself shamelessly against him, letting the pleasure build faster than it ever had in her life.

She was this close to exploding against him when he groaned and pulled back. She couldn't stop the moan escaping her lips the second she was denied. Her hips moved forward without thought, trying to reestablish the delicious contact.

Brock dropped his head, breathing heavily, sweat dotting his forehead. "Fuck, Brianna, one more second and I was going to embarrass myself right there in my pants."

"That was going to be mutual," she laughed.

He looked up at her and the hunger in his eyes stopped her heart. "Your bedroom, now."

She was about to lead him there when he swept her up into his arms and carried her down the hall. He set her down, standing, at the foot of the bed. Brock ran his hands down either side of her body, his palms molding to her curves as his gaze followed. "So damn beautiful."

His expression turned dark and his voice shook.

"Oh my God, Brianna, I almost lost you. The entire time all I wanted to do was rush past everyone else and grab you up and get you to safety. It was torture having to wait, and then you tried to kill me by insisting that Twila go before you." His voice cracked on the last words.

"You don't know what I'm gonna say, and even if you did, it's none of your business," Sonny told his daughter.

Brock gave Brianna a squeeze. "I'll be just outside."

When he and Sonny had walked a little way down the hall toward a small waiting room, Brock started. "I apologize for not coming to you before proposing to Brianna."

Sonny waved him off. "The fact that you're apologizing, and it's to me and not to her father, tells me some of what I need to know about you." They reached the empty waiting room and Sonny gestured for Brock to go in first. When Brock turned to look at him, the pain was back full force in his eyes. "I could only save one of them."

"Sir?"

"My biggest failure in life. I love every person in that room. They are my family and my family is everything. I thought if I could help my sister's children, I could make up for not saving *her*. I love the boy in that bed. But I had to choose when they were younger which one I could save and I saved Brianna." He held up his hand, preventing Brock from protesting. "I know Brian made his choices and he chose to run away over and over. But there came a time that I realized that if I didn't focus everything I had on Brianna, there was a good chance she'd run off with him into the same trouble and I'd lose her, too. The fact that she felt she needed to hide her talents from us—from me—makes me realize she was running away this whole time too, just in a different way."

"Sonny, she loves you and she respects you. She told me that. Brianna just had this idea that her taking up the fiddle would somehow hurt you, that she needed to hide it in order to keep it."

Sonny nodded. "And that's why I wanted a word with

you. Brianna thinks about everyone around her first, to her own detriment. I need to know that you aren't someone else that she's taking under her wing." He held his hand up again to silence Brock's next protest. "I think you're a good man. But I can see you carrying your own burdens, son, and I don't need to know what they are. I just need to know that you aren't looking to Brianna to fix them, or you."

Brock held his anger in check. Sonny wasn't attacking him. They were both on the same page—protecting Brianna. "You're right about me carrying some burdens, but that's where it ends. I'm not expecting Brianna to take them away, or carry them for me, or to fix me. But she does all that anyway, just by being in my life. And right now, my focus is on helping her in any way that I can. I'm here for *her.*"

Sonny appraised him. "She's gonna wanna stay at that bedside today. She'll give up everything she's worked for to sit beside a man who's hurt her time and again. He may or may not ever wake up, but she'll stay and wait as long as it takes."

"And you're wondering if I'll let her."

Sonny nodded once.

"I know it's her nature to do that, to stay and support him. In the end, it's her decision, that's all I'm gonna say. But it's not gonna stop me from encouraging her to go back to the festival and take her shot. So tell me this. If we go back in there, are you also willing to tell her she doesn't have to stay? That her family has her back, that someone else will be here to let her know the second Brian wakes up, if and when?"

"Of course. And it's still gonna take both of us to convince her to go and I'm ready for that fight too."

Brock reached out his hand for Sonny to shake. He was not a little guy, but Sonny's big bear paw still managed to engulf his hand.

"We have a deal. Told Brianna I liked you. You're proving me right in my judgment, son."

Brock smiled. "I'm honored, sir."

"Welcome to the family."

"That honors me, too."

Sonny started to turn and leave when Brock said, "There's just one more thing you're wrong about, sir."

Wariness filled Sonny's eyes. "What's that?"

"You're saving them both. Right here, right now."

Sonny winced. "I...we'll see."

* * *

They left the waiting room in time to catch Brianna's parents looking for Brian's room. They'd gone right past it and they were continuing in the wrong direction.

"Luna," Sonny called. She turned around and gave him a look of pure anguish. She was clutching an old Teddy bear. Both she and her husband looked sober for a change. Luna ran down the hall and into Sonny's arms.

"It's our fault," she sobbed. "If we hadn't bailed him out, he'd be safe. He'd be in jail, but he'd be safe."

Sonny rubbed his sister's back. Brian reached them and he laid a hand on Luna's shoulder. He held something haunted-looking in his eyes as his gaze shifted from his wife, to Sonny, to Brock.

"Let's just go in and see him, Luna, okay?" Sonny said. "We're not gonna assign any blame." He turned her around, keeping an arm across her shoulders. Brian and Brock trailed in their wake. The man was looking around like the same person who beat up his son might suddenly materialize.

"Something wrong, Brian?" Brock couldn't help himself.

The mellow vibe Brian cultivated evaporated completely. "My son is in a coma in a hospital bed and you're asking me that?" he snapped.

"Just looking out for Brianna. Your daughter."

"Brianna's fine, Brianna is always *fine*," Brian said. "Her uncle sees to that."

"Glad someone did."

Brian turned and stopped Brock with a hand on his chest. Brock looked down at the man, who suddenly realized what he was doing and removed his hand. He smoothed his hands down his own shirt. "You don't know anything about our family so just stay out of it, soldier." He spat out the last word.

"Sailor. It's sailor. And I know enough to think that there's more going on here."

"My son had a little heat on him, sure. That's what happens in our business. If the government weren't so busy tryin' to regulate us taxpayers out of our business and paid attention to the criminal element around here—"

This time, Brock stopped Brian. "What criminal element?"

"All of 'em, man." He gestured as though the hospital hallway was full of thugs. "We can't bank, did you know that? Banks won't let us set up accounts even though we're legit. Afraid of running afoul of the feds. That means we do business in cash and it's got no safe place to go. My son takes care of us, his mom and me. Sometimes that means he gets in trouble."

"So you do have people after you?"

"Man, we always have people after us. Do you know how many times we've had to evade assholes waiting to rob us after hours? Finally got an armored truck to carry the money. My son protected us before that. People, they want revenge sometimes. Probably this time, that's what happened." He wiped his eyes.

"Do you have any names?"

"No, man."

"What about Jerold Glass?"

Brianna's father looked genuinely confused. "What about him? Guy's in jail, right? I said no, man, I don't have any names. Could be anybody."

"Oh my God!" Luna cried out when they got to the door. She broke from Sonny's grasp and ran to the bed. "Oh, my baby boy! Mama is so, so, *so* sorry." She laid the Teddy bear on his chest then picked up his hand and started kissing it. Claire went to her sister-in-law's side and put an arm around her. Sonny went straight to Brianna and hugged her. Watching them, a nasty look crossed Brian Senior's face.

"Now what's your problem?" Brock asked.

"Why is my brother-in-law comforting my daughter like that? *She's* fine. She's not part of this at all. She turned her back on us, chose her uncle's family over her own."

Fuck you. "She chose stability over a couple of children in adult bodies who never took care of her is what you fucking mean."

Brian's head whipped around, but again, he took

Brock's measure and backed down, probably the only smart move he'd made that day. "I'm keeping an eye on you."

"Likewise."

Brock went to Brianna and pulled her in close while April approached Sonny.

"The doctor was here while you guys were gone," she said quietly. "We confirmed Brian's identity. He was found—" April choked back a sob—"by a good Samaritan in a ditch by the side of the road. He was basically dead; they had to restart his heart right there. In addition to the beating, there were a ton of drugs in his system. They've detoxed him, I guess. Now we just wait."

Brianna sniffled and Brock squeezed her. She looked up at him. "I need to stay here. I need to—"

"You can't give up your chance." Brock stroked her hair.

"I can't just leave him." Tears rolled down her cheeks.

Sonny stepped closer. "You aren't leaving him, Little B. We're here. Your parents are here. They're not gonna leave his side; we'll make sure of it. You've gotta live *your* life. You aren't your brother's keeper." Her uncle touched her cheek. "You've done enough sacrificing for this family."

"I never sacrificed anything," she protested.

"You're wrong. You've sacrificed so much. Don't sacrifice your music."

"You're uncle's right, Bri," Brock said. "You have a gift that needs to be shared with the world. There's a lot of darkness out there and when you play, that darkness retreats, just a little bit. The world needs that. *You* need that."

Brianna looked back at the hospital bed. She bit her lip, still indecisive.

Sonny stroked her hair. "Someone will let you know the minute anything changes."

She looked back at her uncle. Finally, she nodded. Brock breathed a sigh of relief.

April looked back and forth between her uncle and Brock. "Did you and Brock have a nice conversation out there?" she asked Sonny.

"We did."

"You all done checking his teeth?"

Sonny grinned. "I'm done checking his teeth."

"They got coffee stains?"

"I wouldn't have let him back in here if they didn't."

April patted her father on the arm. "Good Papa." She hugged Brianna. "Now you two get outta here. We got this."

CHAPTER 23

When Brock and Brianna got back to the festival, the news had already spread about Brianna's brother. Brock kept a close eye on her mood as well-wishers told her how sorry they were. He didn't miss the side-eyes a couple other people gave her and the way they avoided going near her as they whispered to each other. He did his best to make sure she missed seeing that. The last thing she needed was some sort of bullshit reinforcement that she was less than anyone else.

Brianna soaked up the positive attention, much to Brock's relief. She kept up a brave face, assuring everyone that she was ready to perform that night and thanking them for their support. God, his woman was strong—Brock knew how much she was hurting inside. He'd make sure she had a safe place to land in his arms that night, where she could sleep or cry or talk, anything that she needed.

Anthony was especially kind when he found them. "Hey, Brianna, I'm so sorry. I talked to the folks in charge and they're willing to let us practice in the farmhouse on the grounds, so you can have some privacy if you'd like."

"Oh, that is so considerate. Thank you for asking." She took a moment to deliberate. "I appreciate the gesture, but you know, I think I'll be okay out here." She nodded to herself. "Yeah. I want to stay connected to everyone else at the festival."

Anthony beamed. "Wow. You have come such a long way this week. I would've thought you'd jump at the chance for privacy."

Brianna's smile looked surprised. "I guess I have." She glanced up at Brock. "Thank you. You're the reason."

Brock shook his head. "Nope. I'm not taking that credit. It's all on you, Lifesaver."

Brianna laughed as Anthony looked puzzled. "My new nickname," she told him. "From the van situation." Her cheeks reddened.

"It fits." He grinned. "Now, since you've got a show to put on tonight, I suggest we get started going over your songs. I have a few last suggestions. Wanna practice by the river?"

"Sure, sounds good." Brianna stood on her tiptoes and gave Brock a kiss. "I know you need to patrol, so I'll see you in a while?"

"Of course. I just need to check in and then I'll be back."

* * *

Brock entered the security station where Kyle, Jake, and Wolf waited. They were with Sargent Williams and three officers from Boulder—Tom Hicks, Sylvie Madden who

Brock recognized from police dog classes at Watchdog, and another officer Kyle introduced as Frank Morris. Valkyrie sat patiently in the corner, watching the men.

Officer Morris started with an apology. "There is no excuse for Brian Taylor to have gone missing and I'm not here to offer one. I'm only here to give my apologies for our slip-up. As soon as Mr. Taylor wakes up, we'll be getting a statement from him. In the meantime, we're still trying to find the records of the officers who took him to rehab."

Fat lot of good that does Brian Brock thought, but he bit back his comment. He couldn't help but notice Officer Madden giving Morris a little side-eye as well.

"*If* Brian wakes up," Brock said. "I just got back from the hospital and he's in a bad way."

"I'm sorry to hear that," Officer Madden said. "We'll get to the bottom of this. The problem is, the officers were in plainclothes, and Brian's parents don't remember getting names or badge numbers."

That was news to Brock. From the looks on Kyle's, Wolf's, and Jake's faces, it was news to them, too.

"Which brings up the possibility that they weren't cops at all," Officer Hicks said, glancing at Morris. "In the meantime, we're here to keep an extra eye on the contestants, given everything that's occurred this week," he continued. "Backstage, we've got extra security, along with officers in plainclothes roaming the crowd."

Kyle crossed his arms. "What about Jerold Glass?"

"What about him?" Morris asked.

"Is he talking?"

"I can't speak to that at the moment. My focus is on the festival today. But I'll let you know the minute I know anything." He looked at the other officers. "We don't like what's going on, either. Glass was flying completely under our radar and we'll be continuing our investigations into that."

"Damn straight we will," Sargent Williams added.

They went over the rest of the day's plans before the officers cleared out of the station, leaving the Watchdog team with Sargent Williams. The man looked exhausted and angry.

I know Glass isn't in Lyons proper, but dammit, he's still in my territory."

Kyle laid a hand on the man's shoulder. "We had the best looking into him, and it still took some digging. Don't put all of that on your shoulders, George."

"I have to, son. This is my town and my responsibility. I've requested more support from Boulder County but we'll see if we get it."

"My team is here for you."

"I appreciate that. In the meantime, I've got my own eyes and ears inside the department." He lowered his voice. "One of them just walked out of here. Word is, your friend Gina is making a lot of people nervous."

"Spooky does that," Jake said.

"I'd love to know the names of the people who are jumpy around her," Kyle said.

"You'll get it," Williams said. "And you'll let me know what she has to say once she does get in to Glass?"

"Affirmative," Kyle said.

Williams took his leave.

Kyle ran his hand through his hair. "I don't like any of this. It just keeps getting bigger and uglier." He looked at Brock. "How's Brianna holding up?"

"She's strong. Right now she's practicing for tonight."

"I'm going to tell you, she's a favorite to win," Jake said.

"Is that according to Rachael?"

"That's according to everyone, brother."

* * *

Walking the festival grounds, Brock would've never known anything was amiss. People were having fun, music was in the air, and cloud cover brought the temperatures back down. Brianna was safe. Gina would get in and Jerold would talk. Brian was stable. Even Jake, Wolf, Caroline, and Rachael looked more relaxed. But Brock couldn't shake the feeling that everything was wrong. The air felt tense and charged like it did before a thunderstorm.

Late afternoon, Brock grabbed a couple of cheeseburgers and a greasy cone of fries from the food vendors for an early dinner and found Brianna with Anthony sitting in a couple of folding chairs in the shade behind the pavilion.

She smiled up at him, then looked at the food. "Oh, thank you, but I'm so nervous I don't think I can eat." She turned to Anthony. "You want my burger?"

Anthony laughed. "Not a chance. That one's yours. Get some food into you before the performance. You don't want to pass out in the middle of your set."

She shook her head and looked at the burger. "I'll do my best."

"You're going to do great tonight. I have all the faith in the world in you." Anthony stood up from his folding chair and nodded to Brock, then headed toward the food vendors.

Brock took the empty chair. "He's right. You're going to kick ass." He handed her one of the burgers and offered the cone of fries.

She snatched a fry and bit into it. Then she took two more. "Maybe I am hungry after all."

"That's my girl." He watched her unwrap the burger and take a small bite. "Before you ask, Brian is still stable."

Brianna nodded. "Luna texted me."

"I notice you always call your parents by their first names."

"They insisted on it from when we were young. Something about how it collapses the artificial power structure of families. I think it just takes away their sense of responsibility." She shrugged. Then she looked up at Brock through her lashes. "Someday I want to be called Mom."

His heart skipped a beat. "By how many kids?"

Her cheeks flushed. "You're saying that's okay by you?"

Brock leaned forward and kissed her. "More than okay."

"Three."

"Three kids?"

"Yup. I want three. I liked the dynamic of three with me and my cousins." She tilted her head. "Sounds good?"

"Sounds perfect." He grabbed her hand. "Never really thought I'd get a chance to be a dad." Brock kissed her fingers. "So, thank you."

"And we'll bring them here every year." She looked around at the passing crowds. "No matter where we end up." She looked back at him. "Would you be okay with moving?"

He looked up at the red cliffs over the treetops. "I like it here. I can't understand why Sean ever wanted to leave. I didn't think I'd feel that way, but I do." He looked at her. "But, I'll go wherever you want me to. Wherever your career takes you."

She raised her eyebrows. "Let's not get ahead. I haven't gotten any nibbles like Amber and Twila have."

"Doesn't mean you won't. Hey, whatever happens, I'm with you."

She smiled and looked around again. "It's funny. I've been trying all my life to get away from here and now that it's a possibility, I'm feeling nostalgic. Like I don't want to leave."

"Lyons has a lot going for it. It's beautiful."

"And this week has taught me that maybe I'm not quite the outcast I once thought I was."

"That, too."

A volunteer came running up to them, her ponytail swinging back and forth. "Hi, sorry, but Brianna? It's time to get ready. There's a photoshoot and stuff backstage."

They stood. "Take your burger," Brock said. "You know what Anthony said."

"Right. Thanks." She started off, looking unsure and a little dazed.

"Hey, wait." Brock reached for her arm and pulled her into his embrace. "Just want you to know I love you. I'm excited for you, and for the life we're starting together."

"I love you, too," she said, her eyes shining. "Thank you for coming into my life."

They kissed and Brianna went off with the volunteer. Brock finished eating and headed toward the stage. Sonny had texted him too, saying that Luna and Brian had agreed to stay bedside so that Sonny and his family could come and support Brianna. Brock wanted to find them and make sure they were able to get up close. The other guys on the security team communicated back and forth on the comm, and all was well. Only a few more hours to go before the last performer took to the stage and finished the show.

On his way up front, he spotted Alex in the crowd. He almost didn't recognize his teammate outside of the kennels at Watchdog.

"Alex," he called and the man turned around.

"Hey, Badger." They shook hands.

"Decided to check out the festival, huh?"

Alex chuckled. "On the recommendation of someone who said I'd love it." He looked around, trying to spot someone. "I'm just hoping I didn't get, um, stood up."

Brock raised his eyebrows. "Dog! You dating someone?"

"Um. Maybe. It's...complicated. Maybe I'm just reading too much into things."

"But you're hopeful."

Alex nodded. "I am that."

"Good luck, brother."

Brock moved on until he saw Sonny's broad shoulders and head above the mass of people.

"Sonny, over here." Brock waved until he got the man's attention. Sonny didn't have any trouble making his way through the crowd that parted for the big bear of a man, making it easy for Claire, April, Kevin, and Hannah to follow.

"Follow me up the side here," Brock said. "I have clearance for us to get up close." They got to the front of the stage where VIP chairs had been set up behind the barrier. People were already taking their seats, including Jake, Arden, Wolf, and Caroline. Brock noted Kyle's absence—the man was not about to relax until the festival was over.

The Taylor family divided up into two rows, Hannah, April, and Kevin sitting in front of Brock, Claire, and Sonny. They'd barely sat down when the announcer came out to a round of applause and named off the finalists. The judges took their places in chairs on the stage and the final round began.

Brianna was third to perform, right after she and the other finalists accompanied Twila for her performance. She already looked like a superstar to Brock's eyes. The woman stood with poise and confidence, the opposite of the shy, insecure woman he'd listened to the first time. You'd never know anything was wrong in her life, the way she smiled and started right in.

Brianna Taylor, world-class fiddle player. I was right about you. Brock's heart swelled with pride for his woman. *My fiancée* he reminded himself.

Beside Brock, Sonny watched in wonder as he listened to the first song. Brianna played a riff and his face broke into a huge smile. "There she goes throwing in a little of Stravinsky's Violin Concerto into the middle of a Bluegrass song. No way." He shook his head. "Hope the audience caught that."

"You really know your music," Brock said.

Sonny gave him the biggest smile he'd seen out of the man yet. "And Brianna knows my favorites."

She finished her set with 'Riversong for a Badger' and the crowd went wild. She took her seat at the side of the stage with the other hopefuls. As the banjo player took her place at the mic, Brock's cell buzzed with a message from Kyle:

Need you at Sgt. Williams' office now. Spooky got through.

Shit. Brock looked over at Jake. He and Wolf were already standing up, having gotten the same message. He excused himself and stood up, too. Sonny gave him a worried look but Brock waved him off. "Work call. If I don't get back in time, cheer Brianna's win extra-loud for me." Sonny smiled and nodded at that and Brock, Jake, and Wolf left, headed for the closest Watchdog SUV and the police substation a few minutes away.

"What've we got?" Brock asked as he jogged into Williams' office. He was surprised to see Gina Smith, aka Spooky, there with Kyle and Williams. Brock had only met the woman in passing at Watchdog, as her home base was with their parent company in Los Angeles. She'd brought her dog, Fleur, with her. Apparently, the two were practically inseparable.

"Brock, Jake." She nodded at the two men, her chin-length bob swaying with her head movements. "And you must be Wolf." She extended her hand and Wolf shook it. "I've heard good things."

"Likewise," Wolf said. "Tex speaks highly of you."

She nodded again. "He helped get me in to talk to Glass. The man is scared. I only needed the carrot and not the stick I was expecting to use. Here's what I've got." Gina set a recorder on Williams' desk and hit play.

Jerold's voice rose from the device. "...Business took a downturn, so I had to do something. I was contacted and made a deal with a supplier. Ran coke, heroin, pills, all through transporting the cars."

Gina's voice joined his in the recording. "And did Brian Taylor work for you?"

"Brian worked for me, sure. He was my distribution guy locally."

"Through his parents' dispensary?"

"Maybe. Yeah, I don't know where. I don't *want* to know where."

Gina paused the recording. "He's lying there. Someone scares him more than I do."

Williams grunted. "I can tell you who scares Glass more than you." He tapped the recorder. "Does Boulder have a copy of this?"

Gina shook her head. "They wouldn't let me record anything. Searched me and everything. And of course I obeyed, didn't I?" She smiled. "I'll make sure *you* have a copy," she added.

"I appreciate it. Fucking gangs outta Denver, that's who scares him more than you. I know they've expanded north. I've been telling Boulder this for a year. They tell me I'm watching too many crime shows on Netflix. They think I'm Andy Griffith. Fuck 'em. The gangs are moving in on us with their damn drug trade and shaking down the local dispensaries."

Fuck. Brock thought back to his conversation with Brianna's father earlier. Before he could speak up, Gina hit play again and Jerold's voice continued.

"So long as Brian was moving product, that's all that mattered to me." He paused. "Then this week, everything went to shit, of course. My luck."

"What happened?" Gina asked.

"Fuck. You said we have a deal?"

Gina's voice oozed sympathy. "Of course. I'm not after you, honestly. You aren't the real problem. You're just trying to make ends meet in a tough economy. I want to go after the real criminals."

"Hell, yeah, I'm not a criminal. I'm an independent thinker. You can see that, can't you, sweetheart?" he cooed.

In Williams' office, Gina snorted. On the recording, she said, "Of course I can. That's why I'm here to help you. Tell me more," she purred.

"So Brian came up short this week and gave me some lame-ass excuse. I told him to fuck off, I wanted my money or my product back. Next thing I know, one of my cars is stolen."

"You think it was Brian getting revenge?"

Jerold's voice paused again and Gina mouthed the word *lying*. "I'm positive."

"I'm confused though. He must not be working alone because he wasn't the one who stole the car. That was two other men."

Another pause, during which Gina indicated Jerold was lying again. "Sweetheart, he's got friends among the old hippies around here. Probably a couple of them did it."

"The video showed a couple of young-looking men."

"Probably their grandkids then, how the fuck should I know?"

"Okay, I'm sure you're right." Gina's recorded voice sounded placating, while Gina-in-person simply looked amused. "So, Brian is angry at you and steals a car. Tell me about the van. I have a source that says you were poking around the vans by yourself. Why did you sabotage it? To get back at him through his sister?"

Another long pause. Gina spoke to the others over the silence. "At this point, his eyes are shifting back and forth like he's watching a tennis match. He's obviously trying to figure out which story is going to do him less harm—admitting to sabotaging the van or passing it off on someone else."

Jerold finally spoke again. "That wasn't me. I didn't sabotage the van."

She hit pause. "This time, he's actually telling the truth."

"Then who? And why?" Kyle asked.

Gina gave him a thin-lipped smile and hit play.

"So are you telling me that Brian was behind the sabotage, too?"

"Positive. Who else would it be? That's why I was checking the vans, to make sure they were okay. But this asshole stopped me before I could check 'em all."

"You could've told someone your suspicions and the accident wouldn't have happened." Gina's voice came through calmly.

"*My* van was fine, so fuck it." He paused again while Gina said, "At this point, he's just caught himself looking bad."

Jerold's voice picked back up. "But I probably could've prevented the accident if I hadn't been interrupted. That's on Brock Jones, not me."

"Fucker," Brock said.

"And the gun?" Gina's voice continued. "You pulled a gun on Mr. Jones."

"Are you stupid? That's because he's in on it too, can't you tell? I had to get out of there."

She stopped the recording. "He devolves from there, claiming that Brianna and Brock were keeping tabs on him for her brother. Oh, and so was Rachael. The man's a pathological liar and trying to save his skin."

"So who is he really protecting?" Kyle asked.

Brock interrupted. "Whoever is shaking down the dispensary." All eyes turned to him and he repeated the fight he'd had with Brianna's father. "You're right, George. Brian is tied up with one of the gangs out of Denver. It's just a matter of knowing which one."

"Whoever it is, Glass is in with them too," Gina said. "But he won't give me a name and I'm not sure when I can get back in there. I was pulled out early as soon as he started in on his lying little tirade. Obviously, they were listening."

'That's troublesome too, that they're protecting Glass," Williams said. He scratched his chin. "They've got something to lose if he talks."

"You think that's what this is?" Gina started pacing. "Bad cops?"

"Absolutely," Williams answered. "Starting with the one who 'lost' Brian Taylor on the way to rehab."

Fuck. "And the cops are all over the festival right now and we have no idea who's good and who's dirty." Brock started for the door followed closely by Jake and the others. "They were obviously trying to get something out of Brian. If they're tied up with this gang, they still might be targeting Brianna." In Brock's mind, there was no *might be* about it. "The van was meant as a warning to Brian, and if it took out Glass along with Brianna, they got the bonus plan."

He reached the front door to the police substation when his cell phone buzzed with an incoming call from Luna Taylor.

"Luna. Talk to me," He barked into the phone while the others stopped to listen. He hit the speaker button.

"Brian woke up," she sobbed. "He woke up, but Brianna, she's in trouble. Are you with her?"

It took everything to keep himself from roaring into the phone. "What did he say?"

"He's been stealing money from some bad people and they think Brianna knows where it is."

Kyle was already on his phone talking to the team at the festival. He looked up. "They announced the winner a couple minutes ago and everyone's leaving the stage." He turned his attention back to his phone. "Mack, I want you to grab her and take her straight to the SUV and to Safe-house One on the hill."

Luna was sobbing into the phone. "Save my little girl."

"Luna, I need you to pull yourself together and tell everything Brian said," Brock demanded as he raced for his SUV. "Your daughter's life depends on it."

CHAPTER 24

Sweat trickled down Brianna's forehead from the bright lights and from nervousness. She sat beside Twila on the main stage, holding hands the same way they did in the van. Of course, both women wanted to win, but the camaraderie they'd developed over the week was the most important thing.

Rachael stood at the mic. Lights flashed in the audience as people took pictures. "Over the past week, I was privileged to meet and get to know some amazing musicians and watch their talents blossom. The friendships we all made will last a lifetime. Every person on this stage tonight deserves to win."

She waited for the applause to die down before continuing. "The judging criteria tonight is based on the total number of votes from the audience and on overall improvement. This man started with incredible skill and we've watched him grow throughout the week. Third place goes to Travis Kline on the banjo!"

The audience applauded as Travis stood up and walked to the mic.

"Next, we have in second place a woman who I've come to know and respect over the past week. She's endured some hardships and powered through, and I'm sure she has a bright future in music ahead of her."

Brianna's heart pounded. Second place would be great. Wonderful.

"Our second-place winner is...singer extraordinaire Twila Hart!"

Brianna and Twila hugged before she went up to the mic.

"Now for our first place winner. This is also someone who overcame so many obstacles this week and really, her whole life. Like I said, the criteria was most improved. This woman has had no formal training yet her skill is amazing and has tripled since she got here. We only recently learned that this was also her debut in front of anyone—I mean, *no one* ever heard her play before this week—and now she shines on stage. We all agreed that she's nothing short of a miracle. Our first-place winner is...Brianna Taylor on the fiddle!"

Brianna covered her mouth as the guitarist and mandolin player hugged her. She floated to the mic and got two more hugs from Rachael and Twila. Someone brought out a brand new fiddle case and handed it to her along with an envelope containing a thousand dollars. Rachael leaned in. "Congratulations, Bri. I know this is overwhelming tonight so I'm going to talk to you tomorrow about joining me on tour later this year."

The audience cheered as she stepped up to the mic, hardly believing any of this could be real. "Thank you.

This is unbelievable. I want to shout out to my fiddle sister this week, Amber Ferguson. She's an amazing fiddler." Brianna had to stop while the audience cheered and applauded in agreement. "She deserves to be up here just as much as I do. And not only because of her talent, but because she is also a kind person who actually offered to loan me her fiddle when I thought mine was lost forever." She held up the beautiful new fiddle. "This is yours, Amber."

The crowd went wild. From the VIP section, Brianna watched Amber cover her mouth in shock.

Rachael said a few more things, but the words were lost to Brianna. She saw her uncle and her cousins in the VIP section near Amber, but Brock was nowhere in sight. He promised he'd be there. Maybe he was backstage, waiting? *Oh, God, what if it's Brian?* No, her uncle and cousins wouldn't look so happy if Brian had taken a turn for the worse, right? What if he had to take care of a different emergency? She hoped he was all right as a volunteer led everyone off the stage, Brianna last in line just behind Rachael and the other two judges.

"Ms. Taylor?" A police officer took her arm as she came down the steps to the open-air space behind the stage. He looked familiar, one of the officers she'd seen all week helping with security. She glanced at his badge and recognized the name. "I need you to come with me. I have some bad news."

"Oh, God, is it Brock? Brian?"

"Yeah, it's about your brother. We need to hurry." He maneuvered her quickly to the side toward the private parking lot.

Brianna looked around for Brock. Shouldn't he be

here? "Do you know Brock Jones? I really need to talk to him."

"Yeah, he's waiting for you at the hospital. You need to get there right away."

"Did he text me instead of my family?" She realized her purse was still back in a locker behind the stage. When she tried to turn, the officer gripped her arm tighter as they kept walking. "Wait, I need my purse."

"Someone's getting it for you and alerting the rest of your family. You really need to hurry, honey. Your brother doesn't have much time. We've got to get you there ASAP."

"Oh my God." The world blurred as tears filled her eyes. "Thank you, Officer Hicks."

"My pleasure, sweetheart."

They made it to the private parking lot. Brock's SUV was gone. He must have gotten a message and gone straight to the hospital. But why not wait for her? They walked toward a police car, then went right past it. Another regular car waited, idling. She didn't recognize the driver. Her stomach sank.

"Aren't we taking your police car?"

"Nope, we're taking this one." Hicks opened the back door on the passenger side.

This isn't right.

Brianna tried to pull away. "Stop. I don't understand. Who's that? Who's the driver?"

"Plainclothes officer. Get in." Hicks placed his hand on the top of her head and shoved her into the back seat, then slammed the door. Brianna scooted across the seat and tried to open the other door but it wouldn't budge. She hit the button to roll down the window but nothing happened. Hicks was in the passenger seat by now and the car started to roll.

"The doors and windows won't open."

"Told you, plainclothes car," Hicks said, his voice drained of all warmth.

The driver snickered.

She knew that undercover officers often looked scuzzy, but this driver went a little beyond. His knuckles gripping the steering wheel were taped like a boxer's.

"Let me out!"

The car exited the parking lot, turned in the opposite direction of Longmont, and sped up.

"I said let me *out!*" Brianna grabbed the driver's head, trying to claw at his eyes. Screeching, he slammed on the brakes. Hicks grabbed her arm, turned, and punched her. Dazed, she fell back, only faintly aware that the passenger door had opened and closed and now the back door was opening.

"No." She tried again to get the other door opened as Hicks got in the back seat.

"I wanted to do this easy, but fuck it," he said. His gun was drawn and pointed at her. "Turn around and put your hands behind your back."

Brianna's blood went cold as she did what he told her. "What do you want?" she asked, her voice quiet and even as he cuffed her. "What did I do?"

"Nothing personal. You can blame your brother." A bandana went around her eyes and the world went black. She struggled and he hit the back of her head, filling the blackness with stars.

"She needs to be able to talk," she heard the driver say.

"Not at the moment." A second, bad-smelling bandana

went over her nose and mouth and Brianna lost consciousness.

* * *

She awoke to a horrible headache and someone roughly pulling her out of the car and setting her on her feet.

"Walk, bitch," the driver said, giving her a push. She blindly stumbled on the gravel under her feet before he grabbed her arm and kept her from faceplanting. *It's surprisingly difficult to walk with your arms cuffed behind your back* she caught herself thinking as if it were important. But her brain didn't want to focus on anything beyond that. Because to think ahead meant thinking of the possibility that she wasn't going to get out of this alive. She knew who Hicks was, and she'd seen the driver's face. They didn't let you live when you knew those things.

Brock didn't know where she was. That was a problem too, probably the biggest.

That doesn't mean he can't find you if you stall long enough to give him time.

She liked that thought. She'd keep that one in mind.

Brianna only heard two sets of footsteps, hers and the driver's. Did Hicks not come along? Was he waiting in the car? Around her, she heard crickets and the air was cooler. Tall grass rustled in a light breeze. *We must be higher up somewhere. No river sounds, no cars, though that might be highway traffic off in the distance. How long was I out?* She didn't think they could be too far from Lyons but she couldn't be sure. They were definitely off the beaten path though.

Her brother had been found in a ditch in the hills west of Lyons.

Their footsteps started to echo off something in front of them. The driver stepped forward and she heard a door open. Her toe hit something and she almost fell again.

"Steps, bitch," the driver helpfully informed her. She wanted to ask how many but she was still gagged.

Brianna moved her sandal up along the first step until she had its measure then stepped up. Twice more and she was standing on a porch. The driver pushed her forward again and a new set of arms caught her. Then she was inside somewhere that smelled stale and unused, still bound and gagged and blind. Her head hurt too, and the bandana gagging her tasted coppery. She was pretty sure it was her own blood from the punch to the face.

Another thought—it might be her brother's old blood. This might be the place where they put him in a coma.

Nope, not going there.

Anytime you want to show up Brock, I'm good with that.

The new man turned her and shoved her down. She landed hard on a wooden chair and cried out at the acute pain shooting through her arms and tailbone. She felt a rope go around her chest and pull tight. Her legs were next. *Properly trussed like Aunt Claire's Thanksgiving turkey.* The thought almost made her laugh. If they wanted any information out of her they'd better hurry before she cracked completely.

"All right, Brianna," a different voice said, "Gag's coming off. Scream all you want because no one will hear you. I'll give you one freebie scream to prove it to yourself, but after that, every time you scream, a finger comes off. I don't like screamers."

"I do," the driver said.

"Of course you do, Guapo." The new guy sounded amused.

"Don't fucking call me that."

Someone loosened, then removed, the bandana. The blindfold stayed in place. She wasn't sure if that was a good sign or a bad one. She refused to scream and give either man the satisfaction. She had a feeling that the new guy probably liked that first scream no matter what he said.

"Very good," he said. "So. Are you smarter than your brother?"

"Am I what?"

He chuckled. "Maybe not, huh?" The floorboards creaked as she listened to him slowly pacing back and forth. "That's too bad, because your brother? He's dumber than shit. He thought he could steal from us. Get high off his own supply that he was supposed to be selling for us. He should have stuck with the pot your folks sell, huh? Instead, he stopped turning over the protection money from their shop. That's stealing from us, too. And, trifecta time—he kept some of the money he owed us from what he did sell. Real, real dumb, your brother."

The pacing stopped directly in front of her. She smelled sweat and cologne and mint and realized his face was inches from hers before he spoke. "His dumbest, and I mean a truly, earth-shatteringly stupid move, was to deny it right here, right to my face. But we got past that lie. My associate has the busted knuckles to prove it."

She knew who that was. The driver.

"And we'd been so *good* to your brother. So *nice*. Gave him a bunch of drugs before that, all at once. But then he got stupid again and wouldn't tell me where he hid everything. Can you imagine that? Well, maybe you can. You're his precious twin, huh? Share all sorts of things with him, don't you?"

"Before this week, I hadn't spoken to him in a long time," she mumbled.

"What's that? You speaking without permission, huh?" Fingers squeezed either side of her chin. "You don't do that here, either."

Across the room, she heard knuckles crack like gunfire.

He let go of her face with a shake and went back to pacing. "You like manicures, huh? Lots of women do. Your brother though, he didn't like his. I think we went a little too rough for him, got a little aggressive with it, took too much off the top."

The driver snickered like he had in the car. Brianna swallowed back bile.

"But you know, in the end, it helped. Got him answering some questions. But I'm afraid it was a little late for him and he kinda died there on us."

A full-on laugh came from the driver.

"I say kinda, because from what I hear, your brother is a regular Lazarus. Aren't you lucky, huh?"

Brianna kept still and quiet.

He stopped pacing again. "You can answer that one. Aren't. You. Lucky?"

She nodded, ignoring the tears wetting her blindfold.

"No, you're not."

"She ain't smart either," the driver said.

"Well, we'll just see about that." She heard him crouch in front of her and the smell of sweat, cologne, and mint came back in range. "Before his pulse stuttered and stopped, your brother finally got a little bit smart. He tried to tell us where he kept the money and the product but he was tripping balls by then. But you know what he said? He said he kept it all in a secret place."

Oh, God.

"And he said the two of you went there as kids, huh? Very sweet."

Oh, Jesus. Brian. Why? She and Brock had just been there, and she hadn't seen a thing. How could she have missed it? Was it all tucked back behind a rock or in a hole?

"So that means you know where it all is." He gripped her face again, his fingers pressing her cheeks painfully into her teeth. "I'm going to ask you where that is and you'd better be smarter than your brother and answer me with the truth. You gonna do that?"

She nodded, the bandana over her eyes now soaking wet.

"Yeah? You're going to tell me?"

"Yes," she croaked. This was her chance. Her next words would either buy her time or kill her on the spot. "But the thing is, even if I tell you, you won't find it."

"Really? What does that mean?"

She licked her dry, cracked lips. Copper. "Like he said, it's a secret place. I could tell you where it is and you'd walk right past it a hundred times. And people will see you walking around there, and they'll catch you."

"This is bullshit," the driver said. "She's fucking with us."

"No, I'm not!" She was breathing fast, trying not to hyperventilate. "I'm not. I just know that if I tell you and

262

you can't find it, you'll think I lied and you'll come back here and kill me. I don't want that. I want to live." She sniffled. "I just want to live."

"So what do we do, huh?" A strong mint smell from his breath as he leaned in closer.

"You let me take you to it, you find whatever he has stashed there, and then you let me go."

The driver laughed. She heard him walking toward her.

"I'm serious. I don't care about what's there. You can have it. I'm just trying to get the hell out of town. I finally have a chance and I'm not going to do anything to mess that up. I don't know what you look like. Either of you. It was too dark in the car," she lied. "I don't know who the cop was, either, or even if he was a cop. He was fake, right?"

Someone grabbed her cuffed hands and found her index finger. She felt taped fingers against her skin. "You want me to break her finger or just tear the nail off?" the driver asked the other man over her shoulder.

"No, please! I'm not lying. You know kids, right? They find hiding places where adults can't find them. That's what we did, and you won't find this place. It's...it's in the cliffs over the St. Vrain, okay? Even telling you that, you can't find it on your own, or even if you do it'll take you forever and people will see you. But I can take you right now while it's dark and then I'll forget everything about tonight, okay?"

The longest moments of her life passed before the man said, "Take her. If she's lying and you can't find the stuff, kill her and leave her there. If it's such a secret place, no one will ever find her, right?"

* * *

The driver kept her blindfolded and tied down in the backseat, his only words, "Where now?" whenever he needed new directions. Brianna took him the back way, hoping she was giving Brock more time to figure out where she might be. *He'd have to be practically psychic though.*

Unless...

Maybe Hicks hadn't lied to her entirely. Maybe Brock was at the hospital not because Brian was dying but because he miraculously woke up and told Brock what he'd said to the horrible man about the secret place.

Such a slim chance.

But one she had to take. She'd already bought herself at least an extra couple of hours, right?

Brianna gave him final driving instructions and minutes later, the driver parked near the embankment they'd have to climb to get to the secret back entrance.

"You'll have to take off the blindfold when we get out. I can't lead you up the hill otherwise."

"No problem," he said as he got out of the car. Which told her he considered her a dead woman whether or not they found the stolen money and drugs.

Brock, please.

The car door opened and he dragged her out by her feet. She hit the dirt on her ass and tried not to cry out. The driver turned her over and opened the cuffs. By now, Brianna's arms and hands had gone numb. She moved them gingerly as they filled with needles and pins. He untied her legs next but pinned her legs down. "If you try to run, I'll shoot you."

"Got it."

He let her up and pulled off the blindfold. The night was black around them, the only sounds were crickets and a great horned owl hidden somewhere in the trees. She could barely make out the darker shape of the cliff against the deep blue sky. No other cars were parked along the road.

"Start walking." She felt something poke the middle of her back. "Or I will shoot you."

Brianna waded into the tall grass at the side of the road. If she went slowly, it might take them half an hour from here to the entrance behind the chokecherry. *If* she pushed her luck. She hoped the driver was an awful climber. Actually, she hoped he'd fall and break his damned neck on the way up.

"How long?" he asked.

"Half an hour. Maybe more. It's been a while since I've been up here and it's the middle of the night."

"Don't fuck with me."

"I wouldn't dream of it."

Bam. He hit the back of her head and she went to her knees.

"I said, don't fuck with me, smartass."

Brianna stood up on shaky legs. She kept her mouth closed after that.

When they reached the entrance, she looked and listened for any sign of Brock. The cave inside was pitch black. The only sound was running water.

"This is it," she said.

"Go in." The driver shined his flashlight inside. "This better not be a fucking trap."

"It's not. Who would I have contacted since you took me?"

"Shut up and walk."

Brianna ducked inside. Only the faintest light came through the holes in the cliff. Ravens clucked at her from above. The driver came in behind her with the flashlight. The beam bounced off the walls.

"I don't see anything in here."

"It's just the first pocket. There's a lot more."

"Fuck. We're gonna be here all night." He shone the light at a group of boulders. "Look back there." She looked around the cathedral room, behind every boulder, while the driver kept his gun on her.

"Nothing in here," she said. *And no sign of Brock.*

"Then let's keep moving."

Brianna led him into the next space. The water was louder and the cave a little brighter from the cliff opening over the river. As the driver shined his flashlight, she held her breath, but there was no sign of Brock.

She was a dead woman.

Brock didn't know where she was, or was looking for her in the wrong place, or would come too late. And that would be the worst.

Brianna went to the far side of the space, to the narrow passage that led to the graffiti-covered room. Maybe she could make a run for it, but would she be fast enough?

"I don't see shit in here, either," the driver said behind Brianna.

"It's gotta be in here. There's several places—"

"Yeah, there are. But you know what? I think I'll look

around now without you. Yeah. I think your usefulness has reached its end."

She heard him rack the slide on his automatic. A cold circle of metal pressed against the back of her neck. She had time enough to pray that Brock would never find her body, never feel the pain of failing to save her in the place where he'd proposed.

The roar and flash of gunfire filled the cavern.

And the bullet missed because Brock was there, pulling her to safety as he returned gunfire.

At such close range, the driver had no chance. His body crumpled to the cavern floor.

CHAPTER 25

Brianna woke in Brock's arms before the dawn. Brock had stirred, nudging her out of a light sleep.

"You're awake?" she asked needlessly.

"Yeah. Sorry I woke you." He pulled her closer and kissed her forehead.

"That's okay." She kissed his jawline.

"You haven't been sleeping well," he said.

"Neither have you."

Brock sighed. "I almost lost you. Twice." He rolled onto his back and gazed at the ceiling.

"But you didn't." She went up on her elbow to study him in the pale light from the streetlamp outside her apartment. "You saved me twice. If I hadn't met you, I wouldn't be here."

He nodded but looked unconvinced. "Someone would have saved you from the van."

She rolled her eyes. "But not the cave. You knew right where I'd be and you waited."

"I did know about the cave," Brock acknowledged.

"So, you saved me when no one else could have."

He stared at the ceiling and said nothing else.

After her rescue, she'd learned that her brother had awakened and told Luna to make sure no one went to the secret place. Luna had no idea what he was talking about, but Brock did. Not trusting the police, he, Jake, Kyle, and Wolf went in through the main cavern and waited silently in the dark at the entrance to the second pocket. He'd almost given up hope when he heard Brianna's voice. The driver, Guapo or whatever his name was, was dead. Brianna didn't know what they did with the body after that, and she didn't want to know.

The official story was that Brock, Jake, Kyle, and Wolf found her at the side of the road like her brother and that she had no memory of anything after accepting her award until they found her.

Officer Tom Hicks had gone AWOL and not even Tex could find him. They couldn't find the place where she'd been questioned either, or the second man with the sweat, cologne, and mint smell.

"This is about what's happening later today, isn't it?" she asked with all the tenderness in her heart.

Brock went from staring at the ceiling to looking at her. He ran his finger along her face. "It is. Yeah. You're right."

She bent to kiss his lips. "You've been beside me ever since you saved me. And today, I'm going to be beside you, supporting you."

Brianna thought back over the last couple of days. Facing Brian was the hardest. But Brianna had to speak to him to know why he'd betrayed her. There was no money, no drugs in their secret place—Watchdog had done a

OLIVIA MICHAELS

thorough search, just to make sure. It had to be hidden somewhere else and Brian not only lied but implicated Brianna.

Brian was out of the coma, but that didn't mean he was well. The effects of the overdose, the beating he took, all of it affected his cognitive abilities. Chances were he wouldn't be able to stand trial for a long time, if ever. Their parents were hiring the best lawyer in Colorado to make sure he was declared incompetent.

Brock held Brianna's hand as she approached the hospital room. A guard stood outside, making Brianna's skin crawl. She didn't think she'd ever be able to trust a police officer again after What Hicks had done to her.

"Do you want privacy with your brother or do you want me to go in with you?" Brock asked.

"Come in, please." She squeezed his hand.

"Of course. I'll stay back though by the door. Give you some space to talk."

"You aren't living up to your nickname," she teased him gently, then kissed him. They went into the room.

Brian was awake. He smiled at Brianna when he saw her, tearing at her heart. There was nothing but boyhood innocence in his expression, the same smile he'd give her a thousand times growing up before their lives diverged so drastically.

"Bri," he said, reaching out his hand. After a moment, she took it. His hand was limp and cool to the touch.

"Love you," he said, smiling wider. She couldn't stand hearing the words.

"Then why did you betray me?" A tear slid down her cheek.

270

Brian's expression went from a sweet smile to sheer anguish. "No. I didn't."

"You did. You told those men I knew where the money was and there was nothing there. Watchdog searched, nothing. You don't remember?"

He shook his head slowly as pain gripped his features. He grimaced and closed his eyes.

"You don't remember." She started to let go of his hand and he gripped her fingers.

"*No*," he said loudly. That caused him more pain. He swallowed and said, "Drugs are sold. Money's gone. I gambled it in Central City." He winced. "Couldn't run away. They tried to... Used you. To get to me. To tell them. If I ran... They'd kill Brian and Luna. Kill *you*." Tears streamed down his cheeks, wetting his pillow. "I lied to them, Bri. Knew they'd take me there, find nothing, and kill me. Then they'd leave you alone. Didn't happen like that."

"But why did you ask me about the secret place that night before they took you?" She wiped her wet cheeks.

"Bri," he slurred. "I asked you about the secret place because... Because I had to know. Had to know you didn't go there. Anymore. That you wouldn't find me there. After."

Chills ran down her spine. She'd thought the same thing about Brock finding her. She and her twin had thought alike after all.

Brian squeezed her hand. "Tried to *protect* you but I fucked up. Always fucking up. Love you."

Brianna held back a sob. Brock made a noise behind her but stayed where he was, respecting the moment. She lifted her brother's hand and kissed it. "I understand now. Brian, I love you, too."

He rewarded her with another innocent smile before closing his eyes and falling into an exhausted sleep.

Brianna wiped away her tears. She didn't let anyone see her cry as she and Brock left the hospital. They didn't say a word on the drive back to her apartment. When they got inside, Brock carried her to bed and quietly held her for the rest of the afternoon. They watched the rain from a late-summer monsoon twist in little rivulets down her windowpane. Brianna pictured the secret place flooded with water, washing away any and all traces of what happened there. Cleansing it.

Brock's sigh brought her back to the present. Later today, it would be Brianna's turn to support Brock in every way she could. She rolled on top of him. "I'll be standing right next to you when you scatter Sean's ashes," she said.

"I know, babe. I appreciate it."

How could she tell him that she hoped he could let go of the past once and for all? To stop blaming himself for Sean's death? She hoped he would find peace after today.

* * *

It was perfect Colorado weather—bluebird skies, a light breeze, the occasional white cloud drifting east, the promise of another cleansing afternoon storm. The St. Vrain ran fast and cold and clear as everyone gathered along the bank watched the dancing water, each wrapped in their own thoughts.

It was a day of new beginnings and a day of letting go and saying goodbye.

Brock couldn't believe how good and full his heart felt while at the same time, a great weight pulled down on it. His future had never looked brighter. The woman he loved stood at his side, ready to spend the rest of her life with him. Rachael had put Brianna in touch with her tour manager and she would be joining the band for the North American tour. After that? A shot at recording her own album. He wasn't sure where they'd end up, but as long as they were together, that's all that was important. He'd miss Lyons though.

Brianna stared down at the water intently.

"What are you thinking, babe?" he asked quietly.

"I was thinking about how I've been so eager to leave Lyons, but now? I think I want to stay. I've got nothing left to prove, you know? Instead, I've seen proof that my little town supports me, and I'm ready to accept it. I want to stay close to Brian and my parents for now, too. They're going to need me." She held up her hand before Brock could protest. "I'm not turning down any touring or recording opportunities or giving up my dreams for them, I promise. But, I think I'm learning how to balance what I need with what people want from me." She looked up at Brock. "How do you feel about staying here for a while?"

"I love that idea." A little of the weight pulling on his heart lifted.

Arden stood holding a small box containing some of her brother's ashes. Brock knew this was a difficult day for her, more so than for him, yet she looked serene. Kyle was the reason for that serenity. He held her close and whispered encouragement in her ear. At their feet stood Camo, the military dog who brought them together.

Arden cleared her throat. "Thank you, everyone, for being here today." She looked up at the sky. "Sean loved days like this. They were perfect for being on the river, either wading along the edge, or riding in a tube, or when he was a kid, training the injured hawk he found that summer."

She looked at Brock. "Sean told me so many times that he was grateful to have you as a friend and a teammate and a brother. I know he'd be so happy that you came and saw the river that he loved. That you found a home here." She looked at Brianna with a big smile. "And love. Welcome to the family, Brianna."

"Thank you," she said, beaming. Brock's heart filled with warmth. Yes, this was the place where they belonged.

Arden opened the small box. She offered the ashes to Kyle and Brock. Brianna held his hand as he took the pinch of gray dust and scattered it over the water.

Just then, a hawk flew low over the river. Everyone watched with open mouths as the bird's arc took him up to the cliffs where he landed on a tree clinging to the rocks. He watched them from above before spreading his wings and disappearing into the sky. Camo barked once; a friendly, playful bark as he wagged his tail and watched the hawk disappear.

And with the hawk went the last of the weight on Brock's heart. It felt like forgiveness, but not from Sean— from himself. He didn't need Sean's forgiveness because he suddenly knew down to his bones that his best friend had never blamed him for the events of that day.

Thank you, Sean. I'll always miss you, brother. But thank you for leading me here, where I belong.

"Are you all right?" Brianna asked him.

Brock nodded and looked at her. "Yeah, I am. This place. You." He shook his head. "I feel like a weight has just slipped off my shoulders." Then he smiled a warm, happy smile. "Like I can finally move into the future With you." He kissed her hand. "I love you, Lifesaver."

Brianna gave him a beautiful smile. "I love you, too, Badger."

CHAPTER 26

Alex Hoff

The box appeared right where it would disturb Kyle the most—in the Watchdog Security kennels. The security system did not trigger at any point, and the cameras had been hacked. At first, they thought the footage was looped before realizing it was DeepFake footage complete with all the dogs in sight.

The same dogs who hadn't barked or seemed to mind that a stranger had been among them.

Alex Hoff tried not to think about the possibility that it wasn't a stranger who left the box in his kennel. He knew the Pup was trying not to think that, either, but his body language screamed it. Kyle had no choice—he had to consider the fact that the fortress he'd so carefully built may have been infiltrated by a mole.

The box was done up like a Christmas present, an obvious jab at Kyle's first visit to Colorado. After their munitions expert, Flint, had determined that it wasn't a bomb, Kyle opened it in the presence of the people he trusted the most—Alex, Flint, Brock, Mack, and Gina. He looked inside, flinched, and went ghostly pale.

"No one, and I mean, *no one*, tells Arden about this," he said.

Inside the box was a blue star-shaped Christmas tree topper and an old worn-out Kong. Under these lay two envelopes. One envelope was made of heavy paper with equally expensive stationary inside.

The letter writer had used a fountain pen and had immaculate, fussy handwriting bordering on calligraphy.

Kyle read the letter aloud:

Dear Mr. McGuire,

We have not formally met, though we do keep crossing paths. Usually when that happens it is under unfortunate circumstances. We think you misunderstand our goals and intentions and do not realize that we could ultimately be allies. We, too, want a safe and peaceful place to live and work as you surely must know. The increase in illicit drug trafficking had come to our attention and we were debating our next move when you and the good people of Watchdog Security took care of the matter for us. For that, we are grateful.

However, that placed us momentarily in your debt. We do not savor debt when it is our own, so allow us to rebalance the scales by showing you our reach and our accompanying mercy...

Kyle stopped and touched the blue star. "The last time

I saw this, I was putting it away in a box of decorations that has been sitting in the attic at the ranch." He picked up the Kong. "This is Camo's favorite old Kong from his military days. I thought he'd lost it in the woods, but Arden swore up and down she'd last seen it in our bedroom."

He picked the letter back up and continued reading:

Inside please find photographic proof that we don't have to work at cross purposes. You began the task of wiping out the vermin infesting our fine home and we have continued your work in what we hope is to your satisfaction. As fate would have it, this particular rat was a bit of a turncoat for us as well.

We will be in touch again. Until then, be of good health and cheer.

Sincerely,

The Capitoline Group

Everyone was too shocked to speak. Even Gina looked like she'd been punched between the eyes.

Kyle set the letter aside and picked up the other envelope. It was brown manila, the size of a sheet of notebook paper. Inside were several eight-by-ten glossy photographs of Officer Tom Hicks. In the first photo, he was whole, but by the last, there wasn't enough of him left to identify him as human.

Gina spoke first. "You know we have your back, Pup. Through all of this. Anything you need."

Kyle nodded. "I know."

Meanwhile, Alex's blood ran cold. He feared for the future and safety of everyone associated with Watchdog. But more immediately, he feared for the woman who'd told him of her suspicions of corruption within the police department, and her determination to root it out and put a stop to it. A woman who he was supposed to meet but who'd stood him up and wasn't responding to his texts.

Officer Sylvie Madden.

AFTERWORD

The town of Lyons, Colorado is a real place (Hey, fellow Festivarians!) though I've taken huge liberties with the geography both in town and the surrounding countryside. But if you ever go tubing in the St. Vrain, do watch your backside—those rocks are *sharp*!

Same deal with any people (or dogs) depicted— everyone is a product of my imagination and no one is based on any real person. And finally, while Lyons does host a number of music festivals, the one portrayed in this book is pure fiction.

I've tried to depict as accurately as possible military working dogs and service dogs—their training, their challenges, and their devotion to their people. There is an amazing program called Puppies Behind Bars (PBB) that trains prison inmates to work with dogs who become services animals that can do anything from detect explosives to helping wounded veterans and first-responders with PTSD. This is a win for everyone! I've known a couple of dogs trained in the program and they are simply amazing. So are the people who make PBB happen. For more information, check them out at https://www. puppiesbehindbars.com/

ALSO BY OLIVIA MICHAELS

Watchdog Protectors Series

Protecting Harper

Protecting Brianna

Protecting Grace (Coming Soon)

And more…

Watchdog Security Series

More Than Love

More Than Family

More Than Puppy Love

More Than Paradise (June 2021)

More Than Thrills (Coming Soon)

More Than Words Can Say (Coming Soon)

More Than Beauty (Coming Soon)

More Than Secrets (Coming Soon)

More Than Life (Coming Soon)

ACKNOWLEDGMENTS

First, thank you, Susan Stoker for letting me play in your world!

As always, thank you, Reader, for giving me a chance. I hope you enjoy reading both the Watchdog Security and Watchdog Protectors series and that I can give you a fun little escape from reality for a while. My goal is to create a world that you would love to live in, because those are *my* favorite kinds of books. I hope to see you around on Facebook, Instagram, or join the newsletter at https://oliviamichaelsromance.com/

Caitlyn O'Leary, Riley Edwards, Celeste Fields, Ophelia Bell, Godiva Glenn, Emily, Becca Jameson, Sara Judson Brown, Marsha McDaniel, and Rayne Lewis. Love and gratitude to you all!

ABOUT THE AUTHOR

Olivia Michaels is a life-long reader, dog-lover, gardener, and a certified beachaholic. When she's not throwing a Frisbee for her fur-baby, harvesting tomatoes, or writing, you can find her playing in the surf, kayaking, or kicking back on the sand and cracking open a romantic beach read.

Never miss a release from Olivia Michaels by signing up for the Olivia Michaels Romance Newsletter. Be the first to read advance excerpts, see cover previews, and enter giveaways at https://oliviamichaelsromance.com/

Follow Olivia on BookBub at https://www.bookbub.com/authors/olivia-michaels

Want more? Come be one of Olivia's Lovelies on Facebook.
https://www.facebook.com/groups/639545290309740/

There are many more books in this fan fiction world than listed here, for an up-to-date list go to www.AcesPress.com

You can also visit our Amazon page at:
http://www.amazon.com/author/operationalpha

Tarina Deaton: Found in the Lost
Aspen Drake, Intense
KL Donn: Unraveling Love
Riley Edwards: Protecting Olivia
PJ Fiala: Defending Sophie
Nicole Flockton: Protecting Maria
Alexa Gregory: Backdraft
Michele Gwynn: Rescuing Emma
Casey Hagen: Shielding Nebraska
Desiree Holt: Protecting Maddie
Kathy Ivan: Saving Sarah
Kris Jacen, Be With Me
Jesse Jacobson: Protecting Honor
Silver James: Rescue Moon
Becca Jameson: Saving Sofia
Kate Kinsley: Protecting Ava
Rayne Lewis: Justice for Mary
Heather Long: Securing Arizona
Gennita Low: No Protection
Kirsten Lynn: Joining Forces for Jesse
Margaret Madigan: Bang for the Buck
Trish McCallan: Hero Under Fire
Kimberly McGath: The Predecessor
Rachel McNeely: The SEAL's Surprise Baby
KD Michaels: Saving Laura
Lynn Michaels: Rescuing Kyle
Olivia Michaels: Protecting Harper
Wren Michaels: The Fox & The Hound
Annie Miller: Securing Willow
Kat Mizera: Protecting Bobbi
Keira Montclair, Wolf and the Wild Scots
Mary B Moore: Force Protection

LeTeisha Newton: Protecting Butterfly
Angela Nicole: Protecting the Donna
MJ Nightingale: Protecting Beauty
Sarah O'Rourke: Saving Liberty
Victoria Paige: Reclaiming Izabel
Anne L. Parks: Mason
Debra Parmley: Protecting Pippa
Lainey Reese: Protecting New York
KeKe Renée: Protecting Bria
TL Reeve and Michele Ryan: Extracting Mateo
Elena M. Reyes: Keeping Ava
Deanna L. Rowley: Saving Veronica
Angela Rush: Charlotte
Rose Smith: Saving Satin
Jenika Snow: Protecting Lily
Lynne St. James: SEAL's Spitfire
Dee Stewart: Conner
Harley Stone: Rescuing Mercy
Sarah Stone: Shielding Grace
Jen Talty: Burning Desire
Reina Torres, Rescuing Hi'ilani
Savvi V: Loving Lex
Megan Vernon: Protecting Us
LJ Vickery: Circus Comes to Town
Rachel Young: Because of Marissa
R. C. Wynne: Shadows Renewed

Delta Team Three Series
Lori Ryan: Nori's Delta
Becca Jameson: Destiny's Delta
Lynne St James, Gwen's Delta
Elle James: Ivy's Delta

Riley Edwards: Hope's Delta

Police and Fire: Operation Alpha World
Freya Barker: Burning for Autumn
B.P. Beth: Scott
Jane Blythe: Salvaging Marigold
Julia Bright, Justice for Amber
Anna Brooks, Guarding Georgia
KaLyn Cooper: Justice for Gwen
Aspen Drake: Sheltering Emma
Emily Gray: Shelter for Allegra
Alexa Gregory: Backdraft
Deanndra Hall: Shelter for Sharla
Barb Han: Kace
EM Hayes: Gambling for Ashleigh
India Kells: Shadow Killer
CM Steele: Guarding Hope
Reina Torres: Justice for Sloane
Aubree Valentine, Justice for Danielle
Maddie Wade: Finding English
Stacey Wilk: Stage Fright
Laine Vess: Justice for Lauren

Tarpley VFD Series
Silver James, Fighting for Elena
Deanndra Hall, Fighting for Carly
Haven Rose, Fighting for Calliope
MJ Nightingale, Fighting for Jemma
TL Reeve, Fighting for Brittney
Nicole Flockton, Fighting for Nadia

As you know, this book included at least one character from Susan Stoker's books. To check out more, see below.

SEAL Team Hawaii Series
Finding Elodie
Finding Lexie
Finding Kenna (Oct 2021)
Finding Monica (May 2022)
Finding Carly (TBA)
Finding Ashlyn (TBA)
Finding Jodelle (TBA)

Eagle Point Search & Rescue
Searching for Lilly (Mar 2022)
Searching for Elsie (Jun 2022)
Searching for Bristol (Nov 2022)
Searching for Caryn (TBA)
Searching for Finley (TBA)
Searching for Heather (TBA)
Searching for Khloe (TBA)

The Refuge Series
Deserving Alaska (Aug 2022)
Deserving Henley (Jan 2023)
Deserving Reese (TBA)
Deserving Cora (TBA)
Deserving Lara (TBA)
Deserving Maisy (TBA)
Deserving Ryleigh (TBA)

Delta Team Two Series

Shielding Gillian
Shielding Kinley
Shielding Aspen
Shielding Jayme (novella)
Shielding Riley
Shielding Devyn
Shielding Ember
Shielding Sierra (Jan 2022)

SEAL of Protection: Legacy Series

Securing Caite (FREE!)
Securing Brenae (novella)
Securing Sidney
Securing Piper
Securing Zoey
Securing Avery
Securing Kalee
Securing Jane

Delta Force Heroes Series

Rescuing Rayne (FREE!)
Rescuing Aimee (novella)
Rescuing Emily
Rescuing Harley
Marrying Emily (novella)
Rescuing Kassie
Rescuing Bryn
Rescuing Casey
Rescuing Sadie (novella)
Rescuing Wendy
Rescuing Mary
Rescuing Macie (novella)

Rescuing Annie (Feb 2022)

Badge of Honor: Texas Heroes Series

Justice for Mackenzie (FREE!)
Justice for Mickie
Justice for Corrie
Justice for Laine (novella)
Shelter for Elizabeth
Justice for Boone
Shelter for Adeline
Shelter for Sophie
Justice for Erin
Justice for Milena
Shelter for Blythe
Justice for Hope
Shelter for Quinn
Shelter for Koren
Shelter for Penelope

SEAL of Protection Series

Protecting Caroline (FREE!)
Protecting Alabama
Protecting Fiona
Marrying Caroline (novella)
Protecting Summer
Protecting Cheyenne
Protecting Jessyka
Protecting Julie (novella)
Protecting Melody
Protecting the Future
Protecting Kiera (novella)
Protecting Alabama's Kids (novella)

Protecting Dakota

New York Times, USA Today and *Wall Street Journal* Bestselling Author Susan Stoker has a heart as big as the state of Tennessee where she lives, but this all American girl has also spent the last fourteen years living in Missouri, California, Colorado, Indiana, and Texas. She's married to a retired Army man who now gets to follow *her* around the country.

www.stokeraces.com
www.AcesPress.com
susan@stokeraces.com

Made in the USA
Columbia, SC
20 November 2024